A Streak Across the Sky

Also by Jack Erickson

Novels

No One Sleeps (Nessun Dorma)

Bloody Mary Confession

Thirteen Days in Milan

Rex Royale

Mornings Without Zoe

Short Stories

Perfect Crime

Missing Persons

Teammates

Weekend Guest

The Stalker

True Crime

Blood and Money in the Hunt Country

Published by RedBrick Press

Star Spangled Beer:
A Guide to America's New Microbreweries and Brewpubs

Great Cooking with Beer

Brewery Adventures in the Wild West

California Brewin'

Brewery Adventures in the Big East

A Streak Across the Sky

Jack Erickson

For Lucy

Chapter One

I bumped into her at the Tides and Tea coffee shop one July morning on my way to a new job. I was taking a few days at Cabot's Harbor and had no idea that our brief encounter would change my life forever and bring special meaning to the words *beach house, summer affairs,* and *secrets.*

The weather was blistering hot and muggy. The women in town were wearing skimpy halter tops, short shorts, sandals, sunglasses, and sunburns. The sexy teenagers looked vampy and carefree, and the rest of the women were trying to look like them. Many of them succeeded.

"Excuse me!" I blurted out when my tray bumped a woman's glass of iced tea. The tea spilled down her bronzed arm, giving it the sheen of a Roman statue.

Her damp arm looked so tasty I wanted to put my mouth down and lick off the tea. But I'm a gentleman who doesn't act out on fantasies. At least, I was until I met her.

She burst out a throaty laugh that sounded like a purr. "Thanks for the shower," she said, grabbing her glass to prevent the rest of it from falling on some poor guy's lap.

"Is this how you meet new girls?" she asked. Her blue-gray eyes, only inches from mine, looked like jewels set against her tanned face. Her mouth was turned up in a comely half-smile.

What a funny thing to say. "Not always, but sometimes it works," I said, smiling.

"That's cute," she answered right back. "I'll bet you have more tricks up your sleeve. When you wear sleeves." She gave another throaty purr.

I grabbed a napkin off my tray and dabbed it on her glistening arm. I felt a jolt of electricity when my fingers touched her skin.

"You have a soft touch," she said, watching me stroke her arm. "It feels like you're giving me a massage."

"Let me get you a refill," I said, looking into her eyes.

John Coltrane had been playing over the sound system while I had stood in line, ordered coffee and a Danish, turned around, and bumped into her reaching for a spoon. I couldn't hear Coltrane anymore. All I heard was her voice, like a sultry sea breeze.

"That would be nice," she said. "Iced chai, ginseng and ginger."

I reached for her half-filled glass and kept my eyes on hers. "I'll bring it to you. Where are you sitting?"

She spotted an empty table in a corner facing the beach. "That one over there. I'll save a spot for you."

I signaled to the barista, who took her glass and refilled it. When she handed it back, I put it on my tray and headed to her table. The air conditioning had chilled the coffee shop to the point where it felt like we were inside an iceberg. It was 8:30 a.m., and I sensed a possible interesting diversion in my beach vacation—or not, if she got away.

Her long, bronzed legs were crossed and extended out from a table the size of a chessboard. Her thin sandals revealed toenails painted deep red. She watched as I carried my tray toward her, fingers steepled in a striking pose, her pale yellow shorts hidden under the table. Her full breasts were held in a sleeveless, bronze, gauzy top with thin straps.

She looked like one of those almond-eyed queens etched on a tablet from an ancient Egyptian dynasty: reed-thin, dark-skinned, cropped hair, wearing bracelets and seated on her throne.

"You're new here, aren't you?" she asked as I put her tea in front of her and sat down. Our chairs were only inches apart, but she hadn't moved them. Our arms were so close I could have leaned over and wiped the rest of the tea off her arm. I could sense the warmth from her body so close to mine.

"Yes, I am," I said. "I stop here when I want to spend a couple of days at the beach."

"What's your name? Mine's BJ. Short for Betty Jolene. My mom was from Alabama."

"Dane. Dane Chambers."

She laughed that throaty burst that made my heart leap. "Interesting name. Sounds like you could be a game show host," she teased, sipping her iced chai through a straw. Her eyes, sparkling blue-gray and set off by long lashes and arced eyebrows, had never left mine. "I've come here every morning this week and haven't seen you."

I nodded. "I got in last night and am spending a couple days before I go to Shattuck to start a new job."

"Which beach are you going to?"

I shrugged. "Someplace where there's not a crowd."

"Good luck. It's July. Every Monday, a new crop of families

shows up for a week at the beach. They plop down umbrellas, beach chairs, coolers, beach balls, plastic pails, and shovels, and leave on Sunday, sunburned, kids screaming, Dad and Mom exhausted. They drive home and spend the rest of the year counting the days until they can do it all over again. You going to join them?"

I laughed and bit into my Danish. "Maybe not, if that's what's ahead of me."

She sipped her tea, our eyes still locked in a way that was both alluring and challenging. It was almost like she was taunting me to see who would blink first.

"I stay away from the crowds," she said. "I go to a beach where you see more seagulls than people. I even have a special place where I sunbathe nude."

How do you respond to a comment like that? "Must be far away from here."

She tossed her head over her left shoulder. "It's north of here, past the state park and game preserve. The road is hidden, so most people don't know where it is. We've had a secluded beach house there since I was twelve years old, when my dad bought the place."

I sipped my coffee and tried to gauge if she was going to continue or was waiting for me to respond. She continued.

"He bought an old house that had been there since the forties and rebuilt it into his dream beach house. We spent almost every summer here until Dad moved to Europe. He hasn't been here in a while, and I'm the only one who has a key."

"You come here often?" I asked.

"I spent the winter skiing in Colorado. Then I went to Paris in May to see Dad and his new wife. But I'd rather spend the summer here than in Paris. The museums and restaurants are packed with tourists, and the French treat them like vermin. My dad is French, and our family spent a lot of time over there while I was growing up. Most of my French friends are married now and live in the Paris suburbs. We kind of lost touch, and I rarely see them when I go over."

I said, "I was there a couple of years ago before I went to grad school. We traveled around in a van and spent most of our time in the south before going to Italy for the rest of the summer."

"I love Italy. I should go back again soon," she said.

She sipped her tea and glanced at the clock on the wall. She ran her hands over her tanned arms. Her long fingers were tan and manicured. No wedding ring. Just a bracelet of oval gold bangles that looked Egyptian.

"Want to see the beach?" She looked at me, her eyes only inches from mine. I couldn't look away. "It's going to be hot in a couple of hours, and it would be nice to swim in the ocean before lunch."

Chapter Two

I followed BJ's tan car out of the parking lot going north. It was 9:30 a.m., and the humidity was so heavy the windows seemed coated with sweat. But I lowered my air-conditioner and rolled down the window to smell the ocean breeze. I wanted to get used to the heat if we were going to the beach.

We drove ten miles and turned onto a dirt road beside a grove of scrub pine trees. We drove a couple of miles east until I could see the ocean across the dunes. BJ stopped at a fence, got out, opened it, and motioned me through. A sign on the fence said: *Eastern Flyway Migratory Preserve. No trespassing. US Department of Interior, Wildlife Protection Service.*

BJ got back in her car, drove north another mile, and turned down a narrow road that was ruts in the sand bordered by sea grass and ponds where white cattle egrets and herons stalked on stilt legs. We bumped along the grassy wetlands, dodging potholes and turning around hillocks, until we reached sand dunes. I saw a narrow passage between the dunes and followed BJ until she turned and disappeared. When I reached the dunes, I looked left and saw her driving parallel to the dunes along a pond. I saw the heads of geese and heard them honking in the tall sea grass.

I looked out on a hundred yards of vacant beach and a two-story beach house made of weathered wood bleached gray from sun and wind. The beach house was built in an intriguing nautical design, looking almost like a sailboat. The walls swept up and out, and the slanted roof extended upward. The broad, wide layout made it look as if a wave could sweep the house out to sea and it could sail across the ocean with a mast raised on the roof. It looked intriguing and mysterious.

BJ parked at back corner of the house beside a dune. There was no driveway, just a flat stretch of sand with a rock path that led to a back door large enough for two cars or a boat. She waited as I parked, and I followed her inside.

What might have been a garage looked more like a marine warehouse. One bay held a small sailboat with a lowered mast and three kayaks. Next to them were a motor launch, surfboards, and a rubber dingy. Workbenches and shelves around the sides were crammed with rubber boots, lifejackets, snorkels, fins, scuba gear, crab nets, fishing tackle, bait boxes, and rows of oars.

"My father loves the beach and everything associated with it," BJ said as she motioned around the storage area. "When he's here, he'll use most of this gear in a few days. It's like he's in a frenzy and has to plunge into all water sports."

She shrugged and we moved toward a door leading into the house. "But he only comes here once a year now, and I don't know what to do with his equipment. My brother doesn't even use it when he's here."

I followed behind her as she opened the back door and carried in a grocery sack and stack of mail she must have picked up before I bumped into her. She dumped the mail on a kitchen counter and put the grocery sack next to the refrigerator. She put bottles of wine, cheese, and lunchmeats into the refrigerator and stacked grapes, peaches, melons, and bananas in a large glass bowl.

I stood in the modern kitchen and looked into a spacious area with no walls separating the kitchen from a dining area and living room. Skylights let in enough sunlight to brighten the whole house. The first floor was as open as a tennis court and had a sliding glass door facing the beach. The curtains were open, and I could see the beach a hundred yards away. Not a person in sight, like she said.

I looked up at the second floor, where a wooden railing led to two rooms that divided the front of the house. The doors on the second floor were open, and through them I could see the sky. It was an unusual arrangement that gave me a sense of being on the beach wherever I stood in the house.

BJ came up beside me as my eyes wandered around the interior.

"My dad had a good eye for design," she said. "I've never seen another beach house like this and maybe never will."

"I agree," I said. "It's so open and natural. And warm. I like it."

"I'm going to change into my bathing suit and go to the beach," BJ said, heading to the open staircase leading to the second floor. "Get your bathing suit and change in the guest room there." She gestured to an open door to my left. She pranced up the open stairs and disappeared into a bedroom at the front of the house.

I went back to my car for my beach bag, which held my bathing suit, sandals, tanning lotion, and hat. When I returned inside, I glanced up and saw BJ slipping off her shorts and top and reaching for something on the bed. She was naked and stepping into her bikini.

Chapter Three

My bikini top had sand in it from my time at the beach the previous day. I brushed it off, and granules spilled onto the floor. I went outside to the deck and stood by the rail, shaking out the rest of the sand. I went back inside, put on my bikini top and went into the bathroom to run a brush through my hair. More granules of sand fell into the sink.

Yesterday had been a relaxing day at the beach. I was alone, but I could enjoy myself alone again, something that had been hard for me in years past. It would be interesting to share the beach with Dane today. It had been a long time since I had invited a man to my beach house. Dane seemed playful and had a sense of humor. A little quiet, but he'd lighten up once we got on the beach and he relaxed. He was going to be fun to spend the day with.

I grabbed two fresh beach towels from the linen cabinet and headed downstairs. I yelled at the closed guest room door. "I'm ready, Dane. I'll get drinks and snacks for the beach."

I went to the refrigerator and pulled out hard-boiled eggs, drinks, smoked turkey slices, cheese, and hard rolls from the breadbasket. I washed out the plastic cooler bag in the sink and put in fresh ice cubes. I grabbed peaches and grapes from the fruit bowl and was ready to go. The door to the guest room opened, and Dane came out, adjusting the string on his bathing suit. Red and white with vertical stripes. Good thing it wasn't one of those vulgar Speedo things; I'd have sent him on his way. Probably.

Lean body, a little pale, nice legs, firm shoulders and arms. A tennis player, maybe. Certainly not a body builder; no more of those. He looked a little shy, invited to a beach house by a woman he's known for an hour. It wasn't an aggressive gesture I'd made, but a friendly one. I'll bet he's never had a woman invite him to her beach house before.

"I've got cold drinks and snacks. We'll come back for lunch when we're hungry. Ready for the beach?"

He smiled. A nice smile. I was liking him more and more.

"Here, take the cooler," I said, handing it to him. "I'll carry the towels and fruit. Hope you like peaches. They're fresh from Georgia; I get them from the farmers market every week. Juicy and sweet."

"Let's go!" he said, turning around with a clenched fist gestured to the beach. We headed to the sliding glass doors and stepped onto the slate pavers, hot from the morning sun.

The sun was almost overhead and blazing down on our deserted beach. A few high, puffy clouds looked like cotton balls against the clear blue sky.

Four-foot waves were moving ashore in long curls down the beach as far as we could see. They crashed on the shore, sending lacy surf onto the sand that soaked in when it reached the highest point. Seagulls lazily swirled through the air, squawking and dipping their wings in the breeze. Killdeer skittered across the foam, matchstick legs moving in a blur. They poked their needle beaks into the foamy surf, rushed to another spot, and jammed down again. A wave came up on shore, and they flew up a few feet before settling down again after the wave rolled back into the ocean.

"Here's my favorite spot," I said, dropping the towels in front of a dune and sitting down on the sand. "I came here yesterday and built a sand castle," I said, pointing to a smooth mound the size of a hubcap at my feet. "It was about two feet high when I finished. The high tide left this little bump."

Dane danced over the hot sand, put down the cooler, and sat on the towel I laid next to mine. "Oh! Oh, that sand is hot!" he exclaimed. "Makes me want to rush into the water. I'll bet you come out here every day. That's why you've got such a great tan."

"This week I have," I said, grabbing a peach and biting into it. The juice exploded in my mouth and trickled down my chin. I wiped it off and took another bite. Delicious!

"I opened the house last Monday and spent my time swimming, walking down the beach, and reading. It's so peaceful away from the crowds. I've been coming here every summer since I was a kid. This was my mother's favorite place to spend the summer. We always came here for her birthday, which just happens to be today."

I tossed Dane a fuzzy peach as yellow as the sun. He snagged it in the air and took a bite. Juice squirted out and he laughed. "That is juicy! And delicious. My first peach of the summer." He held it up in triumph, a big bite out of it. He took two more bites, rolling his eyes as the juice dribbled down his chin.

I laughed at his exuberance. "You're like a kid. Eat as many as you want; I've got a whole basket at the house. I'll get more tomorrow. Do you like to swim in the ocean?"

"I grew up in Idaho and mostly swam in mountain lakes. The water's cool in the early summer, but by July it gets warm and turns over in August. You get a green film on the surface, then clumps start to come to the top, and it gets too yucky to swim in."

I opened a can of iced tea and took a drink. "Want a soda or tea? I've also got some water."

"Water, please. That coffee made me thirsty."

"Here you go," I said, handing him a chilled plastic bottle. He opened it and took a few sips.

"Ready for a dip?" I asked, getting off my towel. "It's hot and I want to cool off before I start reading. I'm into a good book and want to finish it today."

I scrunched my toes in the hot sand, straightened my bikini straps, and headed to the surf. "You coming?" I called back over my shoulder.

"I'm right behind you," he said, getting off his towel.

I ran toward the surf, yelling as the first wave came in and rushed across my feet and up to my knees. It was cold but refreshing. I went out a few steps and dived into the next wave coming in. I held my breath, closed my eyes, and felt the delicious Atlantic ocean engulf me. I was free!

Chapter Four

I watched BJ race into the surf, stick out her tanned arms, and dive into a wave before it came ashore. The wave crashed on the beach, and I waited to see her surface. She stayed underwater for a few seconds, and then I saw her head bob up and turn around to face me. She waved and called out, "Come on in; the water's great!" She dived into the next wave and disappeared.

I reached the surf, waded in slowly, and gauged the next wave rolling in. I let it hit me, the cold water splashing over my swimsuit and up my chest. It was bracing and refreshing. The next wave almost knocked me over, but I kept moving out. I looked around for BJ but didn't see her. I dived into the next wave and surfaced behind it. Ahead of me, I saw BJ's head burst out of the water, her wet hair flat against her forehead. She waved at me, a wide smile exposing her teeth. "Isn't this great?"

I swam closer, but she had already dived into another wave that rolled toward me and slammed into me. I fell back, gulped in seawater, and coughed it out. Salt water was running out my nose, and I blew it out. I looked around for BJ but couldn't see her. I swam toward deeper water, and another wave rolled toward me. I dived into it, and it collapsed on me. I came up, coughed again, and looked for BJ. I couldn't see her. What was she? A human seal? She seemed born for the water.

I took a few strokes, swimming over the next wave, moving into deeper water. I could see a row of waves coming in before they formed curls and rolled ashore. The gentle wave motion felt wonderful but put me slightly off-balance. The wave motion below moved me toward shore while I swam against it to go farther out. It was a wonderful, liberating sensation.

The saltwater in my mouth was sour but refreshing. The sensation of swimming in the ocean was exhilarating. My hair was plastered on my forehead, and streams of water rolled into my eyes. I wiped the water away, looked out over the vast ocean, and was struck by how vast and powerful it looked. Waves crashed behind me, but it was peaceful ahead of me. I turned around to look at the beach in both directions, and saw no one. We were out in the ocean alone, fifty feet from shore, with no one to save us if we got a cramp.

I treaded water and reached down to see if my toes could touch sand. They couldn't. I had no idea how deep the water was. The water was cooler below and warmer at the surface. I spotted BJ and was surprised at how far away she was. She was at least fifty yards beyond me, swimming with a powerful stroke, arms chopping the water, head underwater, feet kicking aggressively. She was a strong swimmer. She kept up her powerful strokes, her head surfacing for a breath before she lowered it and stroked farther out. Fifty yards separated us, then seventy five, then a hundred. I could barely see her bobbing head over the waves.

She stopped swimming, pivoted 360 degrees to get her bearings, and began swimming north, parallel to the beach. She was so far out all I could see was the top of her head not much larger than a seal's head. I didn't want her to get too far away, and I started swimming toward her. I was a decent swimmer, but it had been a year since I had been in the ocean. I was impressed by BJ's strength but not confident of my own in the open ocean.

I started stroking on a course parallel to hers, looking up every few strokes to spot her. After she was more than a hundred yards away, she stopped, looked around to get her bearings, and kept swimming. If she went farther out, I would lose sight of her.

I was getting concerned. What happened if she tired and got in danger? I kept my eyes on the top of her head, watching it bob between the waves. I was making up the distance between us. Then I noticed she wasn't moving away. She was treading water and letting waves pass over her.

Then she rotated in a full circle. She looked toward shore, waved to me, then turned to face the open ocean. Her head bobbed over the waves and I imagined how thrilling it was for her to look over the vast ocean far from shore under her own power. She must be having a transforming experience of her strength and courage, giving her such an exhilarating experience being in the ocean and in control.

A waved passed between us, and I lost sight of her. I made a few quick strokes toward her until I got another glimpse of her. She waved at me, I waved back, and she started swimming toward me.

I was tired. I needed to move toward shore. I rolled on my back and stroked underwater, letting the waves push me toward shore. I would be ok, but I didn't feel safe staying in the water.

I turned to face BJ. She was stroking toward me, her head underwater, her bronzed arms chopping the ocean, drops falling from her fingers. The sun was reflecting off the crown of her head like a halo. It was mesmerizing to watch her; she looked utterly at home in the ocean. She was an incredible woman. Why was I so fortunate to be here on the beach with her? I didn't care; I was thrilled to be watching her swim like a mermaid toward me.

I was getting near shore, and waves were pushing me, cascading over my head, driving me underneath. The waves lifted me, crashed over my head, and tossed me toward the beach. It was exhilarating, feeling the force of the waves and my mere 170 pounds powerless against their might.

My feet touched sand. I struggled to stand but another wave knocked me over, tumbling me to the bottom and tossing me on shore like a piece of driftwood. I choked, coughed, and spit out water and sand. I struggled for breath, kneeling on the beach. I was dizzy and crawled up to the dry sand.

I turned and watched BJ swimming toward shore. She hadn't slowed her strokes the entire time in the ocean.

I stood on the dry sand, exhausted but exhilarated at the same time. What a great feeling! Seawater dripped from my body, my feet in the hot sand, and the sun blazing down. I felt gloriously alive, grateful for this incredible experience of swimming in the ocean and watching BJ move through the water like a seal.

I hadn't felt this carefree in years. I wanted to go out, grab BJ from the surf, wrap my arms around her, and give her a passionate kiss she would never forget.

Chapter Five

I was tired as I swam toward shore, my shoulders weakening and my arms going limp. But I felt wonderful from the long swim in the cold ocean, feeling the currents and breathing deeply of the salt air. Was there any better feeling than this?

Dane was onshore, looking tired but showing me a wide grin spread across his handsome face. I let the waves carry me in, keeping my eyes on him. We had looked into each other's eyes at the coffee shop, at the house, and now on the beach. It was thrilling watching each other's every move. I hadn't had that experience in years. I wanted to see more of this gentle man. And he felt the same, I could tell. I liked it that he didn't hide his feelings.

Dane stroked hair off his forehead, moved toward me, and put his arms out to me. I let the last wave carry me in. My feet felt sand, and I ran ashore into his arms.

He kissed me! What a wonderful surprise. His lips were quivering, and I tasted salt on his tongue. Or maybe it was salt from my own. It was erotic, shivering and dripping on the hot sand, his arms around me, and our tongues twisting around each other. I was turned on and wanted to fall on the sand with him. My head was spinning!

Our bodies were clenched together. I could feel his torso push into mine, and I pushed back. Oh, it felt so good, so natural, and so warm. I was breathing hard, our mouths locked and struggling to breathe through my nostrils. The sensation seemed wonderful and bizarre. I started to giggle, air moving noisily in and out of my nose.

I pushed him back and took deep breaths. "Wait. . . wait . . . I can't breath!"

I gulped in air and Dane watched me, a crazy grin on his face like a kid at Christmas. He looked so happy. So was I!

He had looked preoccupied when we bumped into each other at the coffee shop. He was a different man now. A swim in the ocean and seeing each other's nearly naked bodies dripping with water and hot in the sun—was that what it took to ignite passion?

He held me close. "I was worried about you," he said playfully, his arm around my shoulder pulling me closer. We held each other close, water dripping from our bodies, breathing like marathon runners at the finish line. We stood for a minute in each other's arms, stroking each other's warm backs. I could feel my pulse slowing as Dane held me. It was such a delicious, secure feeling. I never wanted to let him go.

Dane took my hand, and we walked up the beach toward our towels. "You were so far out I could hardly see you." His voice was soft and warm. "I was worried you'd get a cramp or something. You're a hell of a swimmer. Where did you get your strength?" He kept holding my hand until we dropped onto our towels.

"I was a swimmer in high school and try to stay in shape. Every summer I come here to swim in the ocean. It's great exercise and does wonders for my emotional health as well. I feel just so . . . free . . . happy . . . when I'm in the ocean. Isn't it great?"

"It sure is," he said, his smile wide and joyful. His eyes were twinkling and alive.

"Isn't it nice to be alone on the beach? It's special," I said, toweling off my face and arms. He rubbed his towel on my back, long strokes down my spine that made me tingle. *Oooh, he could do this more. I loved it*!

I had to slow down. My emotions were racing. My blood was pumping adrenaline and other hormones from my long swim. But I had to relax and get control before we stripped on the beach and had at each other. I took a couple deep breaths and felt my heart slow down. I lay back and felt the warm sand under the towel. I wanted to roll over, hug Dane, and kiss him again. I had to slow down.

Dane burst out a giddy outburst. "We've got to do this again. Swimming was great! Those waves were brutal, but it was so much fun. I haven't swum in the ocean since last year in Florida. I haven't stayed in shape, and it shows. I was huffing and puffing like I had run ten miles."

Slow down. Slow down. I reached into the basket, pulled out cold drinks and handed one to Dane. The sun was warming my body, drying the water on my skin. My emotions were still racing, but I had to keep them under control. I played casual and put on my sunglasses and toweled off my head.

Slow and easy. Let things evolve naturally. It had been a

long time since I had felt such powerful emotions. Desire, lust, call it what you like. It felt marvelous—but risky for me now.

"I got spoiled when I was a kid," I said, sounding casual. "We'd spend most of the summer here, and I *lived* in the ocean. My brother liked sailing, so he and Dad were off most of the time, but I just wanted to play in the sand and swim. I'd rush out every morning, and my mom would have to drag me in for lunch and a nap. I was as brown as an Indian by the end of the summer and hated to go back to school. All winter I'd dream about the beach and count the days until we'd come back."

"Where did you go to school?"

"Mostly in Michigan. Cold, snowy, long winters until we moved to Colorado when I was twelve. I liked the winters there after I discovered skiing. That was almost as much fun as being at the beach."

"Skiing in the winter, ocean swimming in the summer. No wonder you're in such great shape," Dane commented. I could hear admiration in his tone.

"What were your summers like?" I asked, glad to be talking and not letting emotions get us into trouble. There'd be time for that if things progressed. I hoped they did.

"Not as fun as this," Dane said. "I grew up in Idaho, where my dad had a machine tooling company. I worked for him every summer so I could go to college. I hunted and fished, which meant lots of walking. I love the mountains. I fantasized about becoming a park ranger. I was a firefighter in college during the summers, but it was dirty, dangerous work. I had a couple close calls but got out in time."

"That *is* dangerous. Did you jump out of planes?"

"No, that didn't appeal to me. We went to the fires in trucks. We worked in teams, building backfires and waiting for the planes to drop retardant. It was thrilling for a while, but I got tired of spending summers sleeping in drafty cabins, eating lousy food, and not getting sleep for days on end. The equipment was heavy, and sweat pours off of you. I lost twenty-five pounds both summers I worked."

"I don't like fires," I said. "I never could have done that."

"You're not alone. We had a couple women on our crews, but they were pretty weird. They were there for the thrills and liked to get dirty. Some were fearless and did things guys would never do. I didn't like them on my team."

I was getting hungry. I wanted something more than fruit. "Are you hungry?" I asked. "Let's go back to the house and fix sandwiches and come back. I want to read for a while and take another swim."

Chapter Six

I helped BJ fix turkey and cheese sandwiches with lettuce, tomato, and mayo. She took tubs of potato salad, coleslaw, pickles, and salsa out of the refrigerator and put them in the picnic basket. We went back to the beach, sat on the blanket, talked about past summers, and had a nice lunch on the towels, looking out at the waves and enjoying the glorious summer weather.

BJ was curious about my stories of firefighting and growing up in Idaho. I had always thought I had had a boring upbringing, but she was interested in my childhood and my family. She listened carefully, nibbling on her sandwich and dipping into the salads, salsa, and chips. After we finished and put our paper plates in the hamper, she stretched, laid back on her towel, and picked up a book.

"How about a nap before going back in the water?" she suggested. "This is my summer to read Jane Austen, and I love *Pride and Prejudice*. If you don't have a book with you, why don't you get one from our library? It's on the second floor; turn left up the steps and you'll see the door. It's over the garage. You'll see my dad's desk, computer, TV, and walls of books. Find a couple and bring them down."

She opened *Pride and Prejudice* and searched for her place. She put on her floppy hat, fluffed up the sand for a chin rest, and stretched out to read. Her tanned back was brown as cocoa. No blemishes. Smooth and gently muscled, like an athlete. She reached around and unhooked her bikini straps, letting the sides fall to the towel. Her breast was pressed against her towel, ripe and full. Inviting, but not now.

It felt a little strange going back to her house by myself. I climbed the steps and peeked into BJ's bedroom. Her bed was not made; a cover was tossed over, revealing beige sheets. It looked like she had slept soundly last night, woken up, tossed off the covers, and not touched it since. Her king-sized canopy bed had ruffles around the bottom, a thin blue blanket, and fluffy pillows at the head. A Tiffany lamp, a clock, a glass of water, pictures, and stack of books were on her nightstand. And two pill bottles. One prescription bottle of Prozac from a doctor in Seattle. Another bottle of an herbal medicine, St. John's Wort. What was that for?

I squirmed my toes in her soft carpet. The feeling was soothing. I looked into her bathroom and saw a shower, toilet, and long marble counter with two sinks. Pastel-colored bottles of perfumes, lotions, and soaps were lined up against the full-length mirror. Fluffy yellow and blue towels hung from racks.

The wall next to the bathroom was lined with photos. An open closet was at the far end, but I didn't move closer, since her patio window faced the beach. I was afraid she could see me if she looked up. When I had left the beach, BJ had been facing the house.

I left and walked down the carpeted hallway to the library. I entered and saw what looked to be a university study. Two walls with floor-to-ceiling bookshelves. A large dark desk with telephones, trays of mail and publications, a globe, stacks of documents, and family pictures. In front of the desk were two comfortable leather chairs. In the center of the library was an antique oriental rug in faded rose, blue, and green. The setting looked more like a corporate office than a study in a beach house.

I walked over to one of the bookshelves. A middle shelf held oversized picture books of Milan, Cairo, London, Paris, Tokyo, and other world cities. The shelf above had nature and travel books on the Congo, Amazon, Arctic, Russia, China, Australia, India, and National Parks. At eye level were leather-bound classics by Dickens, Hawthorne, Trollope, Melville, Scott, Dickenson, Thoreau, Proust, Hemingway, Twain, and Fitzgerald. The next row held sets of old Arthur Conan Doyle and Sherlock Holmes classics. The top row had books in French, Italian, German, Russian, and Chinese and librettos from Madame Butterfly, Tosca, Zauberflöte, La Traviata, Eugene Onegin, and The Gambler.

I went to the other side and found rows of American and foreign novels, biographies, memoirs, and atlases. One shelf had histories of war from Peloponnesian to Crimean, Hundred Years, War of Roses, the English and Russian civil wars, Napoleonic, World War I and II, Korean, Vietnam, and the Russian and Chinese revolutions. I reached for a biography of Trotsky.

"See anything you like?" she asked.

She startled me and I dropped the book. I reached down to pick it up and saw her standing at the door, floppy hat pushed back, barefoot from the beach.

"This was my father's favorite room. When he was here, he spent as much time in his study as he did on the beach. Did you find a book you'd like? Let's go back and go for another swim."

Chapter Seven

Dane and I finished our second swim of the day, but I didn't spend as much time in the water as I had earlier. I was tired from my previous swim but wanted to wash off the sand and get cool from the afternoon sun. I always like to finish a day at the beach with a last swim to feel clean and fresh. I'd have a shower later, but the last swim was more therapeutic than standing in the shower, shampooing, and washing off all the sand and salt water. I'd looked down to see grains of sand swirling in puddles and push them with my toes toward the drain in a ritual from my childhood. Being at the beach always made me feel like a carefree child. I needed these experiences to become whole again.

I had watched Dane while I had my last swim. He stayed closer to shore, swimming out a few yards, treading water, and watching me taking lazy strokes between the waves. We'd been at the beach several hours already and were sun-drunk and sunburned. It had been fun, and I hated to have it end. I had to send him on his way but didn't want to hurt his feelings. I was going to invite him to come tomorrow.

He was on the beach, toweling off, when I came onshore. I walked up to him, shaking water from my hair, my legs wobbly from swimming. He tossed me a towel and I dried off, wrapping it around my head. I sat down next to him.

"This has been wonderful, BJ," he said. "I can't remember a day I've enjoyed more than today. I feel like a ten-year-old kid again. I can't imagine a more relaxing way to spend a summer day. I see why you love coming here."

I liked Dane's openness. He'd had a good time, and it showed on his face. A little sunburned, sand in his hair, and a warm smile. I felt glad he enjoyed the beach as much as I did. A good sign.

I packed things in the basket and my beach bag. "I'm glad you like it. You know, I'm really spoiled. When I'm on the beach, I too feel like I'm ten years old and can play in the surf all day long. It's a wonderful feeling."

The afternoon sun was heading west toward the horizon. We had a couple of hours of daylight left, but I wanted to have a shower and relax before a light dinner. I had something important to do that night, and I wanted to be alone. Swimming that last half hour, my mind had been wandering, and I was preoccupied with what was ahead of me. I didn't want to rush Dane off, but I needed to be alone. I headed to the house, thinking of the next couple of hours when I'd be alone. I turned around.

Dane followed a few steps behind me, dancing over the hot sand and turning around to watch waves coming ashore. I could tell that he was disappointed to be leaving with sunlight left.

He caught up with me and we walked toward the house, carrying our towels and bags.

"We had a lot of sun today," he said. "I can tell; I got sunburned and my skin is starting to tingle. We need to get some fluids and put on some lotion."

I laughed. "You sound like my dad. He'd say the same thing, and I'd be out the next day playing as hard as I could. I never wanted summer to end."

We reached the patio, brushed sand off our feet, and washed our legs in the outdoor shower.

The air in the house was cool and refreshing. I felt better and headed into the kitchen to get cold drinks. I handed one to Dane and glanced at the clock: 4:45.

"I enjoyed having you here today, Dane," I said. I could read apprehension on his face.

"Thanks for inviting me. You're a wonderful hostess," he responded, leaning against a counter. His face was pink and shiny. I'd get him some lotion before he left so he wouldn't suffer too much tonight.

"It was a delightful pleasure bumping into you this morning, and it turned into such a wonderful time. If it wasn't for you, I'd have ended up on some public beach with kids kicking sand in my face, dodging Frisbees, and trying to find a space for my towel. You're lucky to have this private beach."

"I know," I said, appreciating his kindness. "I invite friends and they never want to leave. I used to have slumber parties with little girls from town. Dad would build a fire on the beach to roast wieners and marshmallows, and he'd tell ghost stories. He'd make up ones about girls at the beach, and something horrible would happen. They'd end up running for the house, and I'd be the only one left. We'd walk up together and laugh about the other girls. The girls didn't know that I knew all his stories and wasn't scared by them anymore. It was so much fun."

Dane nodded and looked down at his toes. "I think I'd better change," he said and headed to the guest bedroom. He closed the door, and I dashed upstairs for a shirt. I pulled my favorite Indian one off the rack and checked the mirror in the bathroom. I had a pink tinge around my eyes and mouth. I'd need lotion tonight when I went to bed. I grabbed a tube of cream for Dane's sunburn and headed back downstairs barefoot, shirt unbuttoned over my bikini. I was tired but happy. A fun afternoon with a nice man. What could be better? The door to the guest room opened, and Dane came out in shorts, shirt, and sandals. He carried his wet suit and the book.

"I didn't have much time to read this afternoon," he said, putting it on a table. "Maybe another time. It was fun swimming and talking to you today. Thanks again, BJ. You've been very hospitable."

"What are you doing tomorrow?" I asked. His eyes brightened.

"I've got a couple days before I go to Shattuck for the interview. I thought I might stick around and do some exploring."

"Have you ever been sailing?" I asked.

"Just a couple times on small boats. Nothing challenging. And it was a long time ago."

"Would you like to go sailing tomorrow? I haven't had the boat out this summer and need to give it a shakedown."

His eyes lit up. "That would be great! I'd really like that."

"Why don't you come about nine tomorrow. Pick up sandwiches and drinks, and we can have a lunch on the boat. Do you have a cooler?"

"It's in my car."

"I have a big one, but I don't take it on the boat. How about sunscreen?"

"I'll get some."

"Here's some lotion to put on your skin tonight. You don't look too bad, but you'll need it if we go out again tomorrow. You'll need sunblock on the boat; the sun is intense on the water."

He was smiling.

"Don't forget a long-sleeved shirt and pants. You need to cover your arms and legs. I'll see you tomorrow at nine."

Chapter Eight

I took a cool shower, lay down on the bed naked, and pulled the sheet over me. My skin felt hot and dry. I was exhausted and couldn't keep my eyes open.

I took a nap and woke up at twilight. I looked outside and saw the fading sunlight disappearing in the west, with the last light moving across the water, the sand, and the house. A quarter moon was coming up in the east, hanging over the horizon. By nighttime, it would rise over the ocean, pass over the house, and set in the west like the previous night, when I had been on the beach at dark.

I was starved. I slipped the Indian shirt over my body and went downstairs. The air conditioning felt wonderfully cool. I went to the refrigerator and took out the remainder of last night's seafood salad and a bowl of cold shrimp and crab. There was a half bottle of chilled sauvignon blanc that looked delicious.

I poured a glass and put it to my lips. The cool wine slid down my throat, and I felt a jolt of pleasure. Aaah, it was delicious: hints of grapefruit, lemons, and . . . mint? Strange,

I hadn't noticed that last night. I took a roll from the bread-basket and put everything on a tray.

I went into the living room and sat at the dining room table facing the beach. My favorite place for dinners, alone or with someone special.

A breeze was blowing across the beach, waving sea oats in lazy swirls. I'd go outside later and walk on the beach before bed.

I finished the glass of wine and poured another. I dove into the salad and devoured it in seconds, stabbing at the greens and forking the tomatoes and cucumbers into my mouth. The crab and shrimp were delicious. I nibbled on the buttered hard roll, chewing and swallowing slowly. The wine was relaxing me, letting me enjoy my solitary meal as if it was a banquet.

I felt so happy with the day. Rather than another day on the beach alone, I had shared it with Dane. He was a nice guy. He didn't try anything funny. He had been on his best behavior all day. Even that kiss coming out of the surf had been nice. It had been sexy and had felt great. But he had known not to take it any further. *Good for you, Dane. You know how to handle yourself around women.*

I was glad I had asked him to go sailing tomorrow. It would be handy having a man on board. If he hadn't agreed to come along, I would not have taken the boat out alone. I knew other guys I could call for a day sail, but none of them could do more than handle the lines and try to make conversation. No, I was beyond that. I wanted to share one of my favorite beach adventures with someone I really enjoyed.

I finished dinner and looked out at the beach. The ocean was turning dark. It was low tide, and shells were piling up in the surf. They'd be gone by tomorrow.

I took the dishes to the kitchen, put them in the sink, and ran water over them. I'd finish in the morning. I was exhausted and needed to do something before going to bed. I knew I'd fall asleep as soon as my head hit the pillow.

I went upstairs to my bedroom and took pictures off the wall. I took them down to the dining room and lined them in a half circle. The family picture in the center, the picture of me, Brad and little Sylvia next, then single pictures of my mother, my dad, my brother.

I got a candle from the dinette and six smaller ones in holders. I took matches and lit the candles after putting them in a semicircle in front of the pictures.

I was mesmerized by the candlelight flickering in the dark dining room. The flames lit up faces in the pictures, and my eyes moved around the semicircle, looking into the eyes of Brad, little Sylvia, Mom, Dad, my brother. Each year I did this ceremony on Mom's birthday. The people in the pictures never aged; they looked as happy and young as they were when the pictures had been taken. I could keep them forever young as they were in front of me.

I felt tears forming and rubbed my eyes. Tears would come, like they always did. I looked forward to them, knowing I could cry openly in front of their pictures. I looked around the circle again and let the tears flow down my cheeks, running over my lip, where I would wipe them.

The faces were blurry through the tears. They were still alive, I was still loving them, we were all together, and life was wonderful. It always was on Mom's birthday.

I blew out the candles, puffing on each one, watching the flame go out and black swirls rise from the smoking wicks. The smell of the smoke was familiar; I recalled it with bittersweet memories. Every time I smelled smoke from candles, I remembered my ritual of looking at these pictures in the candlelight.

The dining room was dark after the candles were extinguished. I left the candles and the pictures on the table and stood up. I went over to the sliding glass doors and went out onto the patio. The stones had cooled. A nice breeze was coming from the dark beach, and I walked toward the water, down to the wet sand where waves were coming. I watched wave after wave coming ashore, washing over my feet, feeling the cold water cover my toes, ankles, and knees. The quarter moon was lying on its side like in a fairytale. Its yellow light shined on the water, sparkling on the waves coming onshore. Stars twinkled in the black sky like little beacons for night voyagers.

The ocean breeze was cool, and the waves were chilly, but my body was still warm from the afternoon sun. I was tired, yet my body was tingling.

I pulled off my Indian shirt, tossed it backward on the sand, and stepped naked into the surf. I was right where I should be, naked in the surf, night sky overhead, waves coming toward me.

I watched the waves, and when I found the right one, I dove toward it, plunging into its inky blackness to disappear in its embrace.

Chapter Nine

BJ drove to the marine yard and waited for someone to open the gate and let us in. An old man wearing a nautical hat and smoking a cigar flipped a lever in the security shed, and the gates opened. He waved to BJ as she drove through, and she shouted to him, "Thanks, Salty. Good to see you again." He gave another desultory wave and went back to reading a magazine and puffing on his cigar.

The boatyard was filled with yachts, sailboats, trailers, nautical equipment, trucks, and open-bay warehouses. An area along one side opened onto a narrow channel where several smaller boats were tethered to a pier. A crew was raising one of the boats onto a trailer with chains and a winch.

Along the channel was a tall open shed where work crews were scraping barnacles and crud off the hulls and repairing decks, masts, and engines.

BJ drove past a showroom with shiny new boats in the window. She pulled up to a building with walls emblazoned with faded nautical advertising and rusting license plates. A large black Labrador dozed on steps leading into the building.

BJ parked, jumped out of the car, and bounced up the stairs, patting the Lab on his head. He lifted his head, looked up at BJ, and uttered a muffled bark. From inside, I heard a voice.

"BJ's here to pick up Lucky. Hi, BJ. We've been waiting for you." She went inside, and I heard animated male chatter and her familiar laugh.

A few moments later, BJ came out with three guys. They walked around the building and disappeared. I got out and followed them. They walked down a row of sailboats on trailers and stopped at one holding a thirty-foot-long sailboat with a white hull, shiny wooden gunwales, and sleek lines. I don't know a thing about boats, but this one was a beauty.

"She's ready for you, BJ. We got her sea-ready for you."

One of the men got in a truck and pulled the trailer and sailboat out of the row. Painted on the stern was the boat's name: Young, Lucky and in Love. I wondered who had chosen the name. It must have been her dad; BJ wasn't that brash. She would have chosen something more subdued.

BJ joked with the guys as they walked around the boat, inspecting and running their hands over the hull. The guys looked like they subscribed to the same fraternity dress code: scuffed work boots, muscle shirts, tattoos, baseball caps, and stringy hair. They had dirt and grease under their fingernails and calluses on their palms. They clearly liked BJ, teasing her while keeping an eye on me, trying to figure out how I fit into her picture. After they circled the boat, BJ moved toward me and grabbed my arm.

"Hey, guys, here's my sailing buddy, Dane. The last boat he was on was a rubber raft in Idaho!"

They howled and slapped each other on the back. One of them said, "He looks like shark bait to me, BJ. Feed him potato chips and beer and see if he swims. There's some big boys out there would like to nibble on him."

His buddies poured it on. "Hey, BJ, I hear they saw a great white around Gull Point last week. A twenty-footer. He probably heard about you bringing your friend."

More howls and hoots. I smiled and BJ motioned me into the truck. She went back to the guys, and they walked around the boat again, pointing out this and that, snapping the lines, slapping the hull, checking off items on a clipboard that one of them handed to her to sign. She shook hands all around, waved at them, and jumped in the truck next to me. "Thanks, guys. You did a great job. I'll take good care of her," she yelled out the window.

BJ drove off slowly, checking the rearview and side mirrors.

"We'll get the coolers and food from the car, and then we're out of here," she said.

She guided the truck back to the parking lot, and I loaded the cooler, grocery sacks, and beach bags into the boat.

I got back in and she drove toward the gate. "Next stop, Otter Creek Landing," she said. "We'll launch her there."

She eased the truck through the boatyard, driving like she knew what she was doing. The guys had moved to the gate and guided her through, one on each side, a third at the front. When she was out of the yard, they slapped the hull and yelled out, "Keep her high and dry, BJ. Let us know if you need help. You got our channel."

She drove down the approach road to the highway, signaled a left turn, and merged into traffic. In moments, we were heading down the highway for somewhere called Otter Creek Landing.

She picked up speed, moving smoothly between lanes, her eyes shifting from left- to right-side mirrors. She had done this before and was confident navigating a truck carrying a sailboat. I never would have tried this without help, but BJ was calm and cool, passing slower vehicles in the right lane, easing back again, and keeping her eye on the trailer. I didn't want to disturb her, knowing she needed full attention for driving.

We passed over a bridge, and I saw sailboats and fishing boats sailing out of a marina. BJ kept driving, and I looked out at the ocean scenery. It was a beautiful morning, light puffy clouds against pale blue skies, gulls flying over the beaches, and sails moving out to sea. The weather was warm but not blazing hot like it would be this afternoon.

I closed my eyes and drank in the tangy salt air. I felt fully alive and lucky to be with BJ. It was going to be another great day with her.

After a few minutes, she gave me an update. "We're a couple miles from Otter Creek. It puts us close to where I want to sail. There's a rock pile a few miles out that's close to the continental shelf. From the rock, the shelf drops a couple thousand feet to the bottom of the Atlantic. Sometimes you can see dolphins and whales. You'll like it."

Of course I would; we could be sailing to Tahiti or Bora Bora as far as I was concerned.

I saw a sign for Otter Creek with an arrow pointing right. BJ moved into the right lane and exited onto a two-lane asphalt road that ended at ocean's edge. We passed a marine gas station, a market with a bait shop, a row of clapboard homes, and a marina with boats tethered to metal piers. Old men wearing grease-stained caps and coveralls stood idly in front of the gas station, chewing tobacco, spitting in the dirt, and scratching their beards.

BJ drove to the landing, turned the truck around in a parking lot, and backed the trailer to the water's edge. The old men observed her deft maneuvering, spitting tobacco juice onto the dirt, and shaking their heads. One reached into a back pocket for a flask, pulled it out, took a pull, and passed it around.

"Get the coolers on board, and I'll get the harbormaster," BJ said, slamming the door and heading to a wooden shed. I got the coolers and grocery sacks from the backseat and put them aboard.

The boat had a rudder tucked beneath, a wooden helm, and a mast tethered to the deck and wrapped in blue tarpaulin. I looked below deck and saw a lower cabin with a door.

BJ came out with a fellow who couldn't have been more than eighteen. Tall and skinny, with dark eyes and a jerky motion. BJ talked animatedly to him as they walked around the boat and checked the trailer hitch. The kid nodded and went back into his shed. BJ got back in the truck, eased it back into the water, and told me to jump on board.

I pulled myself into the boat and sat on one of the coolers. BJ eased the trailer until it was underwater, then called to the kid, who had come back out of the shed. BJ got out of the truck, held the door for the kid, and got in the boat next to me at the stern helm. The kid got in the truck and eased us back into the water. He jumped out of the truck and released the hitch, and we slowly eased away from the landing.

BJ settled behind the helm and flipped switches and buttons. A throaty engine fired up, and smoke belched out from a stern pipe behind us.

"Hang on tight. We're heading out to sea. Tide's coming in."

I got off the cooler and sat on the wooden gunwale to watch her maneuver the sailboat. She wheeled us 180 degrees until we faced the open ocean. The engine revved up, and we began moving over the waves, bouncing up, then down, as we moved farther from shore.

BJ turned her head right and left, backward and forward, guiding the boat down a channel lined with red marker buoys bobbing in the waves. We moved into the ocean, and she revved the motor, picked up speed, and eased into a wider channel that led to the open ocean. The waves slapped over the hull, and we picked up speed. I looked back and watched the marina getting smaller behind us.

Once we were out in the ocean, BJ stopped the motor. "Time to raise the sail," she yelled at me. "This is where you earn your sea legs, sailor boy."

Chapter Ten

Dane helped me pull back the blue tarpaulin holding the sails. I motioned for him to wrap the tarp and put it in the bag. He followed instructions perfectly. *A good sign,* I thought to myself. *He knows how to take orders and will learn quickly.* I didn't want a know-it-all on a first sail, or someone who had his own ideas.

Dane and I worked well together and raised the sail in minutes. I called out to him to check the lines so I could cut the engine and we would be under sail. He followed instructions again, and we were under our own power in no time.

"You'll make a good first mate by the time we're done," I encouraged him, slapping his butt. He jumped and almost went overboard. I had shocked him, but he liked the slap and gave me a gentle pat on my behind. We laughed and hugged briefly. It felt wonderful and natural.

"Put on some sunblock before you look like a lobster. And a long-sleeved shirt. You'll be fried to a crisp if you don't!" I yelled. "And you have a rank, lowly as it might be. First mate."

"First mate!" he said. "Ahoy, I like that title, Cap'n."

Good sense of humor and fair play. We are going to get along working in cramped quarters. Maybe I'll give him another pat on the butt if he continues to follow orders.

I gave him a tour of the lines and told him where to sit while I got us sailing. The wind carried us briskly over the waves. The sun was beaming down, the wind at our backs, the sail full. It was going to be a great day for sailing.

I called out to Dane sitting on the gunwale. "We're going out about ten miles and turning south. We're heading for a pile of rocks past the ship channel. It's called Gull Point. From there, we can drop anchor and go snorkeling. How does that sound, First Mate?"

He shouted over the wind, "Aye, aye, Cap'n!"

Dane wore a sailor cap I had tossed him from below deck. He gripped the gunwale to keep from falling overboard. He was getting his sea legs. I'd know soon if he was going to get seasick.

The ocean was calm with five-foot waves. I scanned the horizon and checked the compass. We were heading east-southeast, about an hour from Gull Point. The boat was handling well, a steady breeze filling the sails.

Dane looked out, his hand shielding his eyes from the sun, his head turning around to take in the full sails moving us across the ocean. The shore was becoming a faint line behind us. In minutes, we'd be out of sight of land. I wanted to see if Dane would notice.

I checked the rigging and was pleased. The boatyard crew had kept it in good shape over the winter. They had told me in April they'd have it tip-top for my July visit. They had tended the boat since Dad bought it fifteen years ago. He had high praise for their work.

I looked back and saw the last sliver of land disappear below the horizon. We were twenty miles out. Dane turned around, put his hands over his eyes, and scanned the horizon to see if he could see land. When he realized that we were out of sight of shore, he looked at me, cupped his hands and yelled, "Ahoy, Cap'n. We've lost sight of terra firma."

I nodded and gave him thumbs up. My eyes scanned the ocean to see who else was in our area. A couple of fishing boats moving toward deeper water, a yacht heading toward shore, and three sailboats south of us. Shipping lanes were out another ten miles, but we'd be on the safe side of them.

I picked up binoculars and scanned the horizon. I could see the tip of Gull Point, and I made a course correction. We hit a choppy patch, and I yelled at Dane to hang on. He secured his life vest and gripped the gunwales. He was doing fine. *I don't think he'll get seasick.*

Dane pointed when he saw Gull Point to the southeast. He raised a hand and cheered. "Is that it, Cap'n? A speck of land by itself!"

I liked his excitement. He was like a little boy, exuberant and emotional. I was pleased he was having such a good time. What a good sport.

I could see with the naked eye the peak of Gull Point. It's not much more than a pile of rocks, with one sentinel rising about thirty feet above the waves and smaller rocks strewn around its base. On the north side was a clearing where weeds and bushes clung to the rocks. Dad had anchored off the flats one summer, and we swam to them, climbing up and walking around the rocks. Gulls and seabirds had built small nests among the rocks, but they were empty, littered with fish bones, seaweed, and driftwood. Dad had jokingly claimed sovereignty over Gulf Point in the family's name; Dad was king and I was the island's princess. He was so funny. I had always loved telling the story of how our family had its own island, even if it was just a pile of rocks with seagull feathers and fish bones.

I hadn't landed on Gulf Point by myself and decided it was too risky for Dane and me alone. I might tell him the story, and maybe we'd land there another time. If there was another time.

We reached Gull Point and sailed around it about fifty yards out. Dane thrust his hand in the air in a triumphant gesture. I sailed east where the shelf rose up, creating Gull Point as the peak of an underground mountain. The water turned from dark blue to black; it was more than a thousand feet below at this point, and deeper if I sailed farther east.

I turned us around and headed to Gull Point. I lowered the sail and tossed over the sea anchor. It splashed and fell about thirty meters. I secured it to the side and looked down at the bottom. The water was dark blue again, and I could see fish swimming lazily below.

I narrowed my eyes until I spotted underwater caves where lobsters, eels, and stingrays hid in the dark. I'd show Dane and see what he thought of these underwater denizens of Gull Point.

"First Mate! Get on your gear; we're going snorkeling below!" Dane was also looking below and lifted his head when I yelled. With his sailor's cap, he looked like an old salt surveying new lands. He smiled a wide, toothy grin. Such a little boy. I really liked him.

"Aye, aye, Cap'n. Ready to go overboard!"

Chapter Eleven

I fell over backward, holding my mask and snorkel. I slammed into the ocean. The cold water stunned me, but I held my breath against the shock. I righted myself, kicked my legs, and started paddling my arms, not knowing where I was going. A cloud of bubbles surrounded me, and I waited for them to rise so I could get my bearings. The water was cold but clear. I could see rocks and sand below, rising up to a shelf slab that became Gull Point. I turned around to check my surroundings.

The bottom looked about thirty feet down. Beyond the boat was a ridge about a hundred yards away where the blue waters turned dark and ominous. *That must be the continental shelf BJ told me about.* No way I was going near that; she said it dropped a thousand feet straight down, with all sorts of sea creatures inhabiting the rocky cliffs.

I kicked my legs and moved away from the boat. I remained below the surface, getting used to breathing through the snorkel and blowing out to clear water that leaked in. I turned my head and saw the hull of the sailboat about fifteen feet from me. I paddled around it and rose to the surface to get air.

I choked as I came up, confused by the snorkel mouthpiece bulging inside my cheeks. I followed BJ's instructions about clearing the snorkel but finally gave up and pulled it out of my mouth. I coughed, spit out water, and looked around. Waves were rolling over me, gently rocking me and moving me away from the boat. I had thought I might be afraid, alone in the ocean, miles from shore, but I felt calm. It was a great feeling!

I looked up in time to see BJ fall backward in the water. I put my head down and saw her explode in bubbles. Spectacular! She clutched her mask and snorkel to her face like she told me to do. After she had fallen several feet backward, she pivoted around and stroked toward the surface, kicking her feet like a trained diver. It was beautiful watching her move through the water as effortlessly as a dolphin. She was born for the water.

She surfaced a few feet away from me, cleared her snorkel of water, and dove below the surface. I looked below and saw her motion to me to follow her as she kicked away from the hull. Her beautiful blue-gray eyes seemed to fill the inside of her mask.

I surfaced, blew water out of my snorkel, and dove to follow her. The cold water that had chilled me moments ago now felt warm to my skin. I swam a few strokes on the surface to see where she was going. I blew out water, took gulps of air, and started stroking toward her, breathing more evenly. It worked, just like she had said. *Breath normally, don't hyperventilate, get used to breathing through your mouth, and keep the snorkel tube open. That way, you can swim for hours if you don't try too hard.*

She was moving away toward the rock slabs rising above the surface. I looked below and saw gray fish swimming slowly in no certain patterns. Their fins fluttered lazily, and their torpedo-shaped bodies moved gracefully through the dark waters. It was beautiful to watch.

BJ looked back toward me, waved, and motioned to me to swim closer to Gull Point. We got within twenty feet, and she gestured with her hand to a formation below us.

I could see dark shadows against the rock. She had said there were caves in Gull Point, and I realized that must be what she was pointing at. She rose to the surface, took a few breaths while treading water, and then did a surface dive and moved down to the caves, bubbles rising from her snorkel. She approached the caves, moving sideways, waving her arms against the current and circling Gull Point.

I surfaced to clear my snorkel, took a couple of deep breaths, and dove below like BJ. She was halfway around the rock as I swam closer. She pointed toward the rocks. I could see the shadows in the openings. Small caves, not much bigger than a postal box. Barnacles and primitive sea creatures clung to the rocks. Wavelike flutes waved in the currents, flowing back and forth in front of the openings.

BJ stopped in front of one opening, waved her hands excitedly, and surfaced for fresh air. She dove and headed straight for the rocks.

I was out of air and surfaced myself. I gulped in fresh air and dove below. I had to see what she was looking at. I swam closer to her, watching her fins wave lazily in the water, keeping her steady. She pointed to an opening and I looked into the blackness.

I didn't see anything except an inky black opening.

Then I saw what she had motioned about. A few inches from the opening was a creature with a snout like a dog. Two beady eyes on the snout peered out at us. From the height and distance between the eyes, the creature had to be long and large. It looked menacing and dangerous. BJ had said that the eels and manta rays inhabiting the rocks had poisonous stingers and swam through the water as fast as sharks.

BJ held her thumb up and nodded. She was happy; she had found her deep sea creatures and shown me where they lived.

She paddled around Gull Point, pointing at similar openings in the rocks. More snouts, more beady eyes peering out at us.

We surfaced for air. She cheered and then gulped for air. Pulling the snorkel out of her mouth, she called out to me, "What do you think, Mate? Feel like Captain Nemo on the *Nautilus*?"

Chapter Twelve

BJ poured more wine into my glass as we sat on her second-floor bedroom patio and watched darkness fall. We had brought a seafood dinner home after returning the boat to the boatyard. Both of us were exhausted from a day of sailing, swimming, and snorkeling in the ocean. What a wonderful day it had been. I couldn't remember a time that had been so stimulating and exhausting. I would remember today for a long time.

Scraps from a lobster bisque soup, a shrimp and crab salad, French bread, and grilled vegetables were on the glass table next to the bottle of wine and two glasses. We leaned back in deck chairs, accompanied by candles lined up on the patio railing facing the darkening ocean. The candles were wax sentinels flickering enough light to eat and look into each other's eyes.

The darkening sky was revealing more stars by the minute. A cool breeze caressed our skin. BJ got out of her chair and said, "I'll get sweaters for us; it's going to get chilly." She headed into her bedroom and came back with an armful of bulky sweaters. I pushed the dishes to the side, and she dropped the sweaters on the table.

"Here's a light brown one that should fit you. The others are probably too heavy. I brought a blanket, too. Let's move to the loveseat. We'll be warmer there."

We pushed the table to the side and moved a wicker loveseat near the railing chair. BJ pulled a bulky tan sweater over her Indian blouse and shorts. She had taken off her bikini when we got home and had changed into the blouse with no bra.

I put on the brown sweater and settled back into the loveseat just large enough for both of us. She tossed the blanket over my lap and sat down, pulling the blanket over herself as well. We tucked the blanket under our legs and felt instant warmth as it blocked the chilly breeze. It was toasty.

"Ooh, that's more like it," BJ said. She reached over, grabbed my hand, and pulled it over on her lap. "Tell me a story about yourself."

I laughed. "A story? What kind of story?"

"Oh, you know, the kind of story you tell when you've met a girl you like. Something cute and a little revealing. You're signaling you're a tough guy or sentimental. We tell a lot about ourselves when we share our stories."

"Mmm, I guess you're right," I said. "But I didn't think it was as calculated as that."

"Maybe not, but it helps people get to know each other."

"Ok, let me think. . ." I felt her pull her legs up against her chest, our hands wrapped in the middle. It felt warm and intimate, as if she wanted protection from real or imaginary storms.

I thought a few moments, tossing over memories from

my childhood, teenage years, college, travels, and adventures. There was one that seemed appropriate.

"Ok, I have a story."

"Good! Tell me. I'll bet you're a good storyteller!" BJ squeezed my hand, and I noticed myself becoming slightly aroused. She snuggled closer to me.

"It was a dark and stormy night . . ." I began.

She laughed. "No, silly. I mean a REAL story, not one you make up."

"No, this one is real. Here I go." I cleared my throat, announcing I was ready for my story. We were looking up at the night sky, relaxed from the wine and good meal, snuggled next to each other, our hands squeezed together under the blanket, when we witnessed a celestial event I'll never forget.

A fiery meteor blazed across the sky, lighting up the night like a bolt of lightning. Halfway across the sky, a fragment split off forming a second brilliant streak that paralleled the path of the first meteor. The twin meteors disappeared in the night sky just above the horizon. The celestial show had lasted two seconds or less.

BJ's squeezed my hand as if she'd been shocked by electricity. "Dane, look at that!" she shrieked. "A shooting star!"

My heart skipped a beat, either from seeing the meteor or BJ squeezing my hand. I was speechless for a second. When I spoke, my voice broke. "Wow, that was spectacular. A double meteor. I've never seen that before."

"Neither have I," she said. "Do you think it means anything? It was so brilliant—and intense."

"And so fleeting," I said, my heart still racing. "It appeared and disappeared in seconds." We looked over at each other, our faces so close I could feel her breath on my face. I was very aroused by her presence and our shared experience.

"I'll never forget this," she said, squeezing my hand again. "I'm glad we saw this together." My heart stirred at BJ's magical mixture of childlike wonderment and sexy womanhood. She put her head on my shoulder and snuggled closer. "Ok, Mr. Storyteller. I'm ready to hear your tale. It better be good. I'll be listening but remembering the meteors." She squeezed my hand again and I squeezed back. It was challenging for me to return to the storytelling mode, but I took a breath and began.

"One of the most interesting people I ever met was on a backpacking trip to Europe I took after college."

"Ooh, I think I'm going to like this," she said. "I know what happens on backpacking trips to Europe. Lots of eager young college kids having their last fling before going home and getting a job. I did it myself and had a fabulous time. Tell me."

"I'm trying," I protested.

She giggled and squirmed in the loveseat. "I'm sorry. I can't wait. Don't skip the fun parts."

"I went with a girlfriend and two other couples. We started in Paris and made our way to Spain, Germany, and Austria on Eurail passes. After a couple weeks, some of the group wasn't getting along. One of the couples was breaking up. We had a meeting at a café in Germany and decided to separate and go our own ways. So my girlfriend and I split off and traveled on our own to Austria, staying at hostels, visiting churches, museums, parks; eating bread and cheese in the parks. You know the kind of thing."

"Sure. I did it myself. It was fun."

"Well, we weren't really boyfriend and girlfriend like you might think, just good friends who dated but didn't want more than a friendship. No sex, just warm and cuddly. We didn't argue and got along better than most couples in love. I knew she had a serious boyfriend back home, and I didn't want to interfere."

She nodded. "Those are great friendships. Girls need guys like that, believe me. Boyfriends come and go. Friends who are guys last forever." She squeezed my hand again, and my heart skipped a beat.

"So, we were going through Switzerland. Money was getting low, and we found ourselves talking more about what we were going to do when we got back home than what we wanted to do in Europe. We stayed at this hostel in Zurich, and I got a bug. High temperature, coughing, tired all the time. I think it was the mononucleosis that I'd had in college. So we spent a week in the hostel. We met this cool guy from North Carolina named Jeff. Everyone loved him. He was funny, sang, played the guitar, and knew Europe like he had lived there his whole life. He was very handsome, and all the girls wanted to be with him.

"Well, he had an eye for my friend, Sue. She was pretty, but not stunning like some of the other girls who came and went in the hostel. Jeff and Sue spent time together while I stayed at the hostel trying to get my strength back. They'd go out in the day, doing tourist things, and would bring me dinner at night and tell me about their day. Jeff was a pre-med student and got me natural herbs he found in health food stores.

"One night he came to me, and we had a long talk. He shared that he had left the US with a broken heart after his fiancée had broken up with him for another guy. He had been devastated and unable to return to school. So he'd come to Europe and traveled for a year. He had kept all this secret until he met Sue and knew he could trust her. He said he was in love with her and wanted to see her again when we all went back. He was so honest and sincere; I could see what Sue saw in him. He said he wanted to marry her. I thought that was a bit much, but I wasn't going to argue. He said he knew how much Sue and I meant to each other, and he wanted to tell me himself about his feelings for her. He also offered to accompany us home."

"That was nice," BJ said. "Did he?"

"Yes, he did. We traveled back to Paris for our return flights. We all flew home, and Jeff bought a ticket in New York to follow me home to Idaho. He met my parents at the airport, and we all went out to dinner. He spent the night at our house. My parents really liked him.

"He left the next day to join Sue, and sure enough, they got married the next year. He went back to college, enrolled in med school, and graduated. Now they have two kids and are very happy. They invite me to their kids' birthday parties, and Jeff writes me letters and tells me how grateful he is for having met Sue through me. To be honest, I've only spent that time with him in Europe, the trip home, their wedding, and a couple visits to Oregon, where they live. But Jeff says I'm his best friend, and he's eternally grateful for my introducing him to Sue."

I stopped, reached for my wine, and sat back. BJ was leaning back in her chair, her eyes closed, but I could see tears trickling down her cheeks. She squeezed my hand again and opened her eyes.

"That's a wonderful story, Dane. Thanks for sharing it with me." She reached over and pulled my face to hers. She kissed me, her mouth open, her tongue searching for mine. My heart was beating so fast I was afraid it would burst through my sweater.

I couldn't help myself. I was telling BJ stories of my life that I hadn't told anyone in years. I was falling madly in love.

Chapter Thirteen

I pulled the bikes off the garage rack Dad had built to keep equipment off the floor and save space for his boats, cars, kayaks, and trailers. Dane helped me put the bikes on the bike rack mounted on my car. When we had secured them with cables, I took Dane by the hand and headed to the kitchen.

"Grab the cooler in the sink and fill it up with goodies from the fridge. I'll get ice from the outside freezer."

Dane went in to wash out the cooler from our sailing trip, and I got out bags of ice, frozen fish, steaks, and vegetables for tonight's dinner from the large freezer in the garage. I took everything inside, put the food in the sink to thaw, and gave Dane a bag of ice.

"Here's ice for the cooler and drinks."

I went back to the garage and took the bike repair kit, pump, and extra tubes off the shelf in case we needed them. I stored them in the back of my car and went back inside.

"I'm ready," he said, zipping up the cooler. "Drinks, fruit, cheese, lunch meats, tomatoes, cucumber, and carrots."

"Perfect. I've got energy bars in the drawer. Grab a handful, just in case." I pointed to the side drawer, and Dane pulled out a half dozen.

We got in my car and headed toward town, keeping an eye on the low clouds moving across the sky. It was hot and muggy, typical July beach weather, even if rain wasn't on its way. The air-conditioner blew out cool air to keep us comfortable before we got on the bike trail. Once we started on the trail, we'd be dripping wet from the muggy weather. But summer heat and humidity weren't going to stop us from a day of exploring the estuary's bike trails and seeing all the wildlife in the preserve.

I pulled off the road at the sign for the state park and game preserve. The bike trail had been paved over an old railroad track that had carried summer tourists and seafood to East Coast cities. I drove inland, entered the state park, and crossed over the first of several small wooden bridges spanning the creeks and waterways.

The park was shaded with scrub pines and tall bushes. The narrow road wound around streams, open water, and tall grass. Egrets, herons, geese, ducks, seagulls, and pelicans flew overhead and swam in the open areas of the estuary.

"This is the largest estuary in the state," I told Dane as we made our way deeper into the park. "It goes inland about twenty miles and links up with rivers that flow into the ocean. There was an old saw mill here in the colonial days, but the area fell on hard times when the logging industry collapsed. When I was a teenager, environmentalists and county officials got together and turned all this into a recreation area. They did a great job. They built a campground—where you see the tops of RVs—miles of bike trails, and bridges crossing over the estuary. Waterfowl nest here in the spring before heading north."

"It's beautiful. The air smells fresh and clean," Dane said.

I pulled into a parking area in a grove of trees, and we got out. We took the bikes off the racks, and I checked the tires, chains, derailers, and brakes. I took one on a quick spin around the parking lot and called out to Dane, "Get your helmet on. We're ready to go! I'll lock the car. You head that way on the trail where that arrow points. The route's marked with interpretive signs all along the way. I'll catch up to you."

I followed Dane, watching him look left and right as we passed over bridges and streams. I let him go ahead, observing how he was experiencing the trail. I had been here countless times, with family and by myself, and always found this a relaxing and therapeutic way to escape my cares and anxieties. The waterways, tall grass, flowing streams, birds, fir trees, and blue skies all did wonderful things to my worn psyche.

Dane pedaled along, not paying attention to me, gazing at pelicans flying overhead, the dark water flowing through the grass, and geese and ducks on the open water. He seemed as captivated as I had hoped he would be. Every once in a while he'd spot a nest in the grass or a furry creature paddling through the water. He'd turn around, wave at me, point energetically, and nod his head in pleasure.

I was glad he was enjoying it. I stayed behind, wanting him to experience the trail by himself without me chattering about what was around each turn. I slowed down, letting him get so far ahead of me that he couldn't always see me.

He kept going, pedaling slowly enough to observe the natural wonders in the estuary. Every once in a while, I'd come around a curve and spot him gazing at the slow-flowing water, turning in all directions to observe everything. One time he stopped and pointed at a dead tree on the bank with a clump of sticks at that top that was an osprey's or eagle's nest. I could tell he was thrilled at having spotted it and pointed it out to me.

I felt so happy. I hadn't been biking on this trail in a year. I knew I would have felt sad being there alone this time. Taking a friend, particularly a new friend, was exciting once again.

I took time to enjoy the estuary, like I had so many times before. I got lost in the beauty, serenity, salty air, cry of birds, and gentle flow of dark water through the tall grass. I felt young again, taking pleasure in the sights and smells and sounds of my happy life when we had spent so much time at the beach.

The sun was hot, beaming down on my tanned arms. Dark clouds were moving across the azure sky. It was muggy, but that didn't bother me or Dane. I felt I could bike all day through this beautiful place. I didn't want anything to interfere with my reentry to the wonderful places I had loved when I was young.

I became lost in my daydreams. I turned a couple of corners, didn't see Dane, and pedaled faster to catch up with him. We had been out an hour. Soon we would come full-circle to a beach picnic area near the car where we could have lunch under a grove of pine trees with a carpet of pine needles as our floor.

I was lost in my reverie when I turned at a grove of trees and saw Dane spilled onto the asphalt, his bike beside him, clutching his ankle. His face showed he was in pain. He rolled on his back, holding his foot in the air.

Oh, no! Dane's hurt! What happened to him?

Chapter Fourteen

BJ was a good sport about my accident. She picked me up, helped me hobble to her car, eased me into the front seat, and gently tucked my swollen ankle into the car with minimal pain. Fortunately, we were only a couple of hundred yards from the parking lot and picnic area where we were going to have lunch. She retrieved our bikes, secured them to the roof rack by herself, and had a great attitude about it all.

In the car on the way to the hospital, I apologized repeatedly and told BJ how foolish I felt. I was in pain, sweat pouring off my forehead, electric currents running up my leg. My ankle hurt so much that I was afraid I had broken something. Despite my grimacing, BJ was upbeat and supportive.

"Come on, champ. Sit back, relax, and enjoy the ride. We'll get you to a hospital and fix you up like new. You're in good hands. We got you before the creatures could come out of the swamp to drag you in."

I managed a weak smile, relieved that she could inject a little humor into my embarrassing situation. She grabbed my arm, squeezed it, and let her hand slide down into my lap.

My hands were gripping my lower leg, but I reached up and grabbed her hand. It was a touching gesture.

"You'll live, sweetheart," she said. "I'm glad it's just your ankle. Nothing looks broken, just swollen like a melon."

She was right. My ankle was the size of a softball, with bruises and a nasty scrape on the outside. It hurt like hell, but I thought her diagnosis was right. I certainly hoped it was.

BJ chattered all the way to the hospital, keeping my spirits up while she told stories of taking spills when she was a girl, falling from trees and car windows, off bikes, and from a second-story window while climbing down a ladder.

"I was a rowdy tomboy until I turned twelve and started to grow boobs. I resisted dresses and frilly things for another year until I started liking the looks the boys were giving me. I exchanged my baseball glove for lipstick and makeup and started to have fun being a girl. But my old tomboy tendencies rear up when I get to the beach. You're seeing me like I really am, swimming, diving, sailing, bike riding every day. Good thing we don't live near mountains, or we'd be putting on crampons and scaling the tallest peaks."

Listening to her made me feel better. At least I wasn't thinking about my own misery.

She continued. "And twenty years later, I'm still in one piece, having adventures every day. All of these sports have boosted my confidence and helped my sense of balance. I haven't fallen in years and have learned my limits. I know when to stop and don't go further. Like snorkeling around Gull Point yesterday. I'd never do that with a scuba unless I had certified divers with me. I don't trust myself in dangerous situations like that. But with snorkels, you're always close to the surface. And did you notice I didn't let us get too far from the boat? I had a line in the water just in case the ocean currents carried us away."

Later that afternoon, I hobbled out of Cabot Harbor's Woodland Hospital with BJ at my side carrying a plastic bag of medications for my sprained ankle. I had felt foolish, explaining to the emergency room doctors and nurses how I had become distracted watching a fish hawk snatch a fish from the stream. I had turned around and was going too slowly when I hit a bump and collapsed, putting out my foot sideways on the asphalt. I fell like a bag of cement on my outturned ankle.

BJ helped me into the car, and we left the hospital parking lot. As we approached the center of town, she turned before we reached the main street leading to the harbor.

"I need to pick up dinner tonight. I don't want to be cooking and taking care of you at the same time. Is that ok?"

"Absolutely. I'm your captive; do with me what you like. You're going to feed me again tonight?"

"I wouldn't miss tonight for the world. I can't resist telling you again and again how funny you looked when I came around the bend and saw you spilled on the trail in that most ungraceful position." She laughed, clearly enjoying my awkward situation.

She turned onto a side street with several restaurants. "Your choice tonight: Indian, Thai, Chinese, Mexican . . . no, let's not do Mexican, do you mind?"

"No. Your other choices sound great, except Chinese. I don't like monosodium and soy sauce."

"How about Thai?"

"Wonderful. My first choice."

She came out of the Thai restaurant ten minutes later with a paper bag holding plastic containers. She put them in the backseat near my crutches and came around to my side of the car. "I need ten minutes to do an errand. Our old family friend Simms had the locks changed last spring after we had workmen at the beach house upgrading the kitchen. I only have two keys, so I need to have some spares made. I'll be right back."

She went into the hardware store on the corner and came back with a brown bag. She tossed the bag in the backseat and drove to the grocery store, where she came out with two sacks.

"We're in good shape now; a couple bottles of wine, juice, drinks, fruit, and a surprise for my wounded patient." She was beaming.

"Mmm, what could that be? Ice cream? Chocolate cake?"

"No, no, then it wouldn't be a secret."

We got to the beach house around six-thirty. It was still warm and muggy, and dark clouds were still moving in from the ocean. "Looks like we'll get that rain tomorrow. Glad it didn't happen today."

She helped me out of her car into the house, my arm over her shoulder while I carried one crutch and used the other to balance myself. She set me on the sofa in the living room facing the sliding glass door looking out at the beach. She brought in the groceries and dinner and got busy in the kitchen. She chatted on about her our day and the people she had seen while shopping.

BJ brought me a glass of pinot noir. She went to the hutch and took out silverware and beautiful Italian ceramic place settings for the table.

After the table was set, she reached into her shorts pocket and pulled out the paper bag with the spare keys. She tore open the stapled bag and dumped the keys onto the tabletop just as the phone rang. As she turned toward the kitchen, the keys spilled onto the floor, flying in several directions. "Oh, damn," she said.

She dashed off to the kitchen to get the phone.

I made a motion to get off the sofa and hobble over to where the keys lay.

"No, no, don't bother, I'll get them," she said.

BJ grabbed the phone and greeted someone warmly. She carried on an animated phone conversation with what sounded like another woman. After a couple of minutes, she begged off, saying, "Can I call you tomorrow? I have a friend over for dinner. The poor guy is nursing a sprained ankle that I'm responsible for. I got him into this mess, and I have to help him recover."

The person on the other line said something, and BJ laughed. "Right. I'll tell you all about it tomorrow. Don't be naughty."

BJ came back into the dining area and got down on her knees to retrieve the keys. She picked them up and set them on the table. She counted them. "Hmm. Funny, I thought I had four. I've only got three here. I wonder if I miscounted. Maybe the hardware guy only made three. I was so busy talking to him that I didn't count when he put them in the bag."

"I heard a tinkle when they fell," I said.

"That was the heating vent under the hutch. I'll bet one went down there. Don't worry about it." She shrugged, put the keys in a drawer, and went back to the kitchen.

"Time for dinner. Need a refill on the wine? I'm starved."

"No, thanks. But will you tell me now what my surprise is?"

BJ grinned: "Mango-banana sorbet. It's my favorite. Hope you like it, too!"

Chapter Fifteen

I helped Dane into the guest bedroom, his weak-side arm around my shoulder while I held him around the stomach.

"It's too hard to get you up the stairs. We can stay down here tonight," I said. Dane had a happy but bewildered look on his face. Probably because I had been so direct getting him into bed two nights in a row.

"I have to take care of my patient," I continued as I set him on the edge of the bed. "Every nurse needs a pleasant bedside manner. Sleeping with my patient is part of the medical services I provide at my house."

He laughed and said, "You mean everyone gets this treatment? What if they stub their toe or get a hangnail?"

I poked Dane in his side and tickled him. "Silly, you know what I mean. Only my *special* guests get the first-class treatment. In fact, if memory serves me, you're the first."

"Well, that makes me feel better," he said as I helped him pull his shirt over his head. He was sunburned from our day on the beach and the sailing. He tugged at his belt, and I helped him. I pulled off his pants, leaving him wearing nothing but his shorts.

"You should get into the bathroom before I tuck you in. I'll help you in there. Then you're on your own, buster."

He guffawed, and we hobbled into the bathroom until he could use the counter to balance himself. I set his crutches inside the bathroom door, left him to do his business, and headed out.

"I'll be right back. I have my jammies upstairs." I dashed upstairs, tossed my clothes on the bed, and reached for my favorite nightclothes, a nightshirt and a pair of footies.

I went back to his bedroom, and he was already in bed, his bandaged ankle elevated and sticking out from the covers. The nightstand lamp was emitting a soft light that fell across the bed.

"Those are nice jammies. Do you have some similar ones for your guests?" he asked.

"I think you're healing fast," I teased. "One more comment like that and you'll sleep out in the garage on the cement in a moth-eaten sleeping bag. You didn't get to see these last night. I thought I'd model them and help you heal."

"I'd sleep anyplace as long as you were with me," he said, a twinkle in his eye.

"You *are* better! Or are the meds making you silly?"

I got in on the other side of the bed, fluffed up the pillow, and looked across at him. The light was behind his head, creating a halo effect. I adjusted my pillow so I could see him better.

"Now that he's tucked in safe and warm, how's my patient—other than a lousy comedian?"

His grin said it all. "I feel a hundred percent better than this afternoon. I think it's your bedside manner. I don't even care if I have a swollen ankle, as long as I get such great atten-tion. Truthfully, you're a fabulous host and a skilled nurse. I see a new career for you if you're interested. What other talents do you have?"

I shrugged. "I don't know. I guess you'll have to find out for yourself." I leaned over and kissed him. We sank down into the sheets, our arms around each other, and lay there kissing tenderly. The only sounds were our breathing and the gentle whoosh of the waves outside. It was heavenly. In this mood, we could get carried away very quickly.

It was too early for sleeping, and I wanted to talk more. After a long, deep kiss, I gently pushed away, fluffed up our pillows, and propped myself up on my elbow, looking down at him.

"You told me a wonderful story last night," I said. "Can I tell you one tonight?"

He looked up, his eyes soft and warm. I was surprised by my forwardness. I didn't know why I was leaping forward with my story, particularly that night. Even though we had been together only a few days, it seemed the right thing to do, considering how well we were connecting. We were becoming closer and more open to each other, a feeling that would have surprised me just a few days previously, before I met Dane. The more time we shared together, the more it seemed I needed to share this with him.

Before he could say anything, I started. "First of all, I have a confession. You're the first man I've been with in over three years."

He blinked as if he had heard a loud noise. "Really! I'm surprised," he said. "You're very attractive and fun to be with. I thought you'd have plenty of boyfriends and have your pick."

"True, it was like that for me awhile back. But I've been 'out of circulation' the last couple years."

Dane looked at me but didn't say anything.

"I noticed you looking at the pictures on my bedroom wall last night."

He nodded.

"You saw some with me and my late husband and daughter."

He blinked and a sad look came over his face.

"Thank you for not asking last night. It would have been too hard to talk about this. It was our first night together, and that might have, you know, changed what happened with us."

Dane nodded and I kept on talking. "I noticed a puzzled look on your face. I hadn't told you I was married before and had a four-year-old daughter. I can tell you now. Do you want to know?"

He nodded, moving closer to me. Our faces were inches apart. I could feel his breath on my cheek. I felt nervous but relaxed enough to tell him.

"We were living in Washington, where I was teaching in a suburban Seattle school." That part was easy. Nothing revealed yet. He didn't seem upset that I had been married and had a family.

"I taught elementary school and loved it. We had a baby a year after we got married, and I took time off when she was born and went back to work when she was two. We were happy. Had lots of friends and a cute home with pine trees, fruit trees, and a garden. Our second-floor bedroom window looked out at Mt. Rainier. We were so happy."

Dane was transfixed. I reached down and kissed him on

the lips, then on his forehead. "I think I'm going too fast. Is this too much to be hearing now?"

He shook his head. "No. I want to hear your story. There's so much I don't know about you. This is important to you, and that means it's important to me. I want to know more about you. I . . . think . . . I'm falling . . ."

I put my fingers on his lips. "Hush. We don't need to say things like that. Not yet. I just wanted to check. Not too fast. There's more for us to learn about each other before we go further."

I cleared my throat and adjusted my elbow on the pillow, looking down at Dane's sunburned face glowing in the light. We were bathed in a soft yellow glow. Outside I could hear wind coming off the ocean, blowing the sea grass and swirling sand across the beach.

He nodded again, and I went on.

"I was pregnant with our second child. A little boy. We were going to call him Nathan. He was going to be born in March. My family was coming for Thanksgiving, and we were having a big celebration at our house, full of little kids, parents, siblings, nephews, nieces. A Norman Rockwell Thanksgiving.

"It was Monday, Thanksgiving week, and we were going shopping after my classes to get the turkey, cranberries, potatoes, sweet potatoes—everything we needed. I was making two pumpkin pies and a pecan pie.

"I was waiting at my school. My husband was picking up Sylvia from daycare and coming at four o'clock. I waited in my classroom, but he didn't come. I locked my classroom door and went to the front office, which was closer to the parking lot. I talked to the principal and secretaries, all excited, but no Brad. We heard sirens. First one, then another, and then more. I waited. Four-fifteen, four-thirty. The secretaries were ready to leave but didn't want to leave me alone. Brad always arrived on time.

"While I was waiting, a teacher's aide came back to the school, parked in the bus lane, and ran into the office. She saw me, her face ashen, and she went immediately into the principal's office. They came out, and the principal told me the aide had seen an accident that looked like Brad's car."

Dane's face turned gray. He knew he was about to hear something terrible. I wanted to go on but didn't want to scare him off.

I lay down on the pillow, looking up at the ceiling. I hadn't told this story in a very long time, and never to a man whose bed I shared. My head was swirling. Why was I putting him through this? I was unloading a grievous story, sadder than most men could handle. I feared he might get up and go in the bathroom to break the tension.

We lay in silence, the only sounds being the whisper of the wind and surf outside the window. A gust of wind or a bird hit the house, making a dull noise. Dane turned so he could see my profile. Out of the side of my eye, I could see him watching me.

"You don't have to go on, BJ. If this is too hard, I can wait."

Tears were streaming down my cheeks. "No, I need to go on." He leaned back on the pillow and waited.

"It was Brad's car. He was hit by a drunken motorcycle driver. Brad's car went into the ditch, and he and Sylvia . . ." I began to cry harder. "Right after the funerals, I had a miscarriage that I believe was caused by my grief." I began sobbing harder and couldn't stop crying.

Dane reached around and enveloped me in his arms. I was sobbing. He held me, moving his body as close as if we were one. His tears fell on my face. I held him close and never wanted to let go.

Chapter Sixteen

I got out of bed at dawn and made my way into the bathroom, using chairs and one crutch to navigate. BJ was still asleep, her face turned to the wall. I wanted to let her sleep. She needed to rest and get up on her own.

I took a robe from the bathroom door and hobbled out of the guest bedroom. Dawn was coming over the ocean, a hazy yellow sun breaking through low gray clouds. I moved from table to chair to stairway with one crutch, managing better than I expected, taking care not to put weight on my bandaged ankle. It was still swollen and was throbbing from the tight bandage. I had taken a couple of painkillers after we got home the previous night and desperately needed more now.

It had been quite a night. We had talked, cried, and kissed each other's tears away. We had cuddled, stroked backs, and hugged so tightly I had thought I was going to crush her ribs. BJ and I both had gotten naked and let our bodies touch, an experience that had felt deeply comforting and arousing. We had made love in slow, smooth motions without talking, our heavy breathing the only sound in the room.

When I had exploded in her, we both had cried out in ecstasy and collapsed in each other's arms, our bodies damp with sweat. We had run our hands over each other, intertwining our moist legs together.

I had felt like I was in a dream, sexually satisfied yet drawn to BJ's incredibly beautiful and erotic body next to me as I drank in the musky aroma of our post-coital juices. She was a vibrant and sexy woman, and I was powerfully attracted to her. More than I'd ever been with any woman.

While I had gazed down at her, she had reached up to kiss me without opening her eyes and then had rolled over to face the wall. When I had heard her breathing deeply, I had rolled over on my back to elevate my ankle. I had stayed awake for a while but finally had fallen asleep, exhausted from our bike-riding excursion, the hospital visit, talking and crying in bed, and lovemaking.

I now hoped she would sleep for another couple of hours. She needed it. I didn't know what she would be like when she woke up.

I looked over at the sofa, where we had eaten dinner, drunk wine, and watched darkness come to the beach before eventually making it into the guest bedroom. I went over to the hutch where I had put my pain pills. I popped a couple in my mouth and gulped water from the glass I had used at dinner.

I reached down for my sandals, shorts, and long-sleeved shirt next to the dresser, where I had tossed them when we had come into the house. As I picked up my shirt, a key fell out on the carpet. It was the sixth key, the one BJ thought had gone down the heating vent. I looked at it and was going to put it on the hutch. But the hutch was several steps away, so I put it in my shorts pocket. I'd give it to her when she got up.

I lay down on the sofa and looked out over the beach, my foot elevated on the armrest. I felt drained and depressed. Such a tragic story BJ had told me in bed. I wanted to cry all over again. We had reached a deeper level in our brief relationship, and I sensed that things would be different when she got up and we started the day. What would come was a mystery.

I tried to get comfortable as I looked out at the beach morning. But I felt restless and thirsty. I got up again, made my way into the kitchen using furniture and one crutch for balance, and poured a glass of juice. I was closer to the bedroom but could hear no sounds. Good. She needed the sleep.

I went back to the sofa, stared at the beach, and thought about the days since we had met. We had had three . . . four wonderful days that seemed to grow more intense the longer we were together. After last night, I sensed we should somehow take a break from each other. I had an important job interview Monday and needed to make my way to Shattuck in a day or so. But my first priority was spending as much time with BJ as she would allow.

I hobbled to the sliding glass door and made my way onto the patio, chair by chair, until I reached the sandy beach. I sat on a flat rock and watched the sun rise, burning off the low gray clouds. Overhead, large white cumulus clouds were forming. It looked like we might have good weather.

I recalled warmly the day we'd spent on the beach. It had been an exciting and new experience to share it with a beautiful woman I had just met hours before. The days between then and now had been even more exciting. But the mood was changed now, and I couldn't imagine spending another casual day at the beach.

Around seven-thirty, I went back inside. The door to the guest room was still the way I had left it. No sound from the room. I lay down on the sofa and again elevated my bandaged leg. I fell asleep in minutes.

I felt a hand on my shoulder and bolted. BJ leaned down and kissed me on the forehead. "Hi, sleepyhead. I missed you in bed. I thought we'd wake up together."

Her eyes looked bloodshot and tired. She came around the sofa sat down next to me. She stroked my head, running her hand down my side. I put my arm around her back.

"I said too much last night," she whispered. "I didn't mean to spill everything. I've had a sad life the last few years, and no one needs to suffer with me."

I sat up in protest. "No, don't apologize, BJ. I'm glad you told me. I know it was very hard to do. But it doesn't change a thing with us. I love you and want to be with you."

She put her finger on my lips like she had the previous night.

"Let's stop talking about what happened last night. That's a lot to put on someone so quickly. Let's get a shower and have coffee. I'm starved."

She led me back into the guest bedroom, and we went into the bathroom. We took a shower together, washing and lathering each other, mumbling gentle words, using soft touches, and giving each other tender kisses. BJ had gotten large white towels and robes for both of us from a closet. We dried off, put on the robes, and went into the kitchen.

She was quiet. So was I.

At the dining room table, we sipped coffee, nibbled on toast and marmalade, and waited for the other to talk. With all that had been said the previous night, the silence felt natural. "How's your ankle?" she asked, looking more awake now.

"Still sore and swollen. I need to take those pills today and keep it elevated."

She nodded. "Do you have plans for today?"

I shrugged. "I have to be in Shattuck on Monday and need to do a little preparation. I don't want to walk in on crutches, but I don't know what I can do about that."

I waited for her to comment.

"I have plans today. This will be our last today together."

I was shocked. That was not what I wanted to hear. "Ok," I said, not knowing what she meant.

"I'm leaving town myself soon and have a lot of things to take care of. If you'd like to stay here the rest of the day, please do. But I won't be here."

"Ok," I repeated, realizing how dumb it sounded. "I'll get a motel room and head north tomorrow. I want to get my bearings in Shattuck before Monday."

"Will you come back?" she asked.

What a strange question to ask after what we had been through.

"Of course, anytime I can. You tell me when, and I'll be here."

"I want to see you again. A year from now. The week of July 20. Come the day before."

"A year! I have to wait that long?!"

She waited a long time before she answered. "These last few days have been wonderful for me. Meeting you was . . .

was . . . like medicine for me. Good medicine. You made me feel alive and like a woman again. I'm very grateful for what you've done for me."

"These days have been wonderful for me too, BJ. But we can't see each other for a full year? I don't want to wait that long. I don't understand."

She sighed. "I know. I know. It will be hard for me, too. But that's a request that I'm asking you to accept. Next year we'll talk again about . . . seeing more of each other."

I still was puzzled but didn't want to argue. I had no choice but to accept her unusual condition.

I said, "Ok, if that's what you want, I'll come back next July. And I won't contact you." She smiled, clearly relieved, and reached over to squeeze my hand.

"Thank you for understanding, Dane. I'll be waiting for you."

Chapter Seventeen

On New Year's Day, I came down the stairs as quietly as I could, not wanting to awaken Jenna. We had gotten to bed late after too much champagne, oysters, prime rib, shrimp cocktails, eggnog, and all sorts of fattening and unhealthy foods. Her parents always celebrated New Year's at the Sun Valley Ski Lodge with their kids, grandkids, relatives, and neighbors from home. We had spent the last New Year's at Sun Valley and had discussed the idea of returning this New Year's and making an engagement announcement after I had settled in to my new job.

Jenna and I had made love last night, the first time in weeks. The champagne, wine, eggnog, and oysters had been a contributing factor. The previous fall, she had started hinting, then openly discussed, and finally complained that our sexual activities had not been satisfactory since summer, when I had taken the new job in Shattuck.

"What happened to you last July? You sprain your ankle and your love muscle goes into hibernation?" she had grumbled after three glasses of champagne the previous night. "Is there a connection between the two joints? I didn't hear about that in anatomy class or from my girlfriends. But something happened to you after you fell off that bike. Are you sure you fell on your ankle and not your groin?"

Ouch. She was right. I had been far from amorous with her since last summer. She had visited me at my new apartment in St. Francis in the fall, and we had been more like friends than lovers. I had showed her around town, and we had gone to concerts, hit the bars and restaurants, met my new friends, and taken drives to the beach. Long drives. But not much time in the sack. Nor had we talked about becoming engaged.

Two times she had come to visit, October and November. She hadn't offered to return in December, saying I could come to Sun Valley with a little more sexual gusto and a marriage proposal. She had told me her mom had been pestering her, and Jenna had had little to say other than that I was in a new job and stressed about doing well. And preoccupied. Who could argue?

Jenna kept bringing up my sprained ankle and the circumstances around it. She knew I didn't have a bike, and I had let it slip that I hadn't recuperated at my motel but at a beach house. Then there had been questions about the beach house, who else was there, how I had met people so quickly that they would invite me to their beach house and take care of me after my accident. I ducked, dodged, feinted, and made up a story about meeting people at a restaurant who had rented a beach house and had invited me on the spur of the moment. It wasn't all that far from the truth, but I had left out important details, and Jenna smelled it.

I had paid attention to the details, knowing that my week in Cabot's Harbor would come up again and that I had to keep my story straight. I'm not a fibber, and the whole experience made me squirm. *Never again,* I promised myself. I knew I'd never make it as a criminal. I'd fall apart the first time I was interrogated.

As a weak alibi, I told Jenna I hadn't been to a gym in months and needed to get back in shape to ignite the old sex spark plugs. She raised an eyebrow whenever I brought it up, but she knew I'd always been physically active. Our best sex had been when I was training for a triathlon and had more energy than any one man should have. Jenna begged me to get back in shape and to be my old self again in bed. A tiger, not a kitten, she kept warning me.

I sat in a soft chair, reading *The New York Times* and looking out the cathedral windows at the ski runs. Jenna's parents' condo had spectacular views of Sun Valley's mountains and ski lifts. I was reading an article on technology exports in the business section when I heard from the kitchen the clink of ice cubes dropping into a glass from a dispenser, followed by water gushing out.

Jenna was in the kitchen. Somehow she had made it down without my hearing her. The business article was good, and my hearing had been tuned to other sounds in the condo, including her younger brother playing computer games in his bedroom. I had missed Jenna's padded feet coming down the stairs and heading into the kitchen.

She came into the living room, wearing her robe and holding a glass of ice water in her hands. She sat down next to me and looked out the window. She drained the ice water and still didn't look at me or speak. I sensed a lateral assault. I put down the paper to prepare a defense.

"Good morning, Jenna. Happy New Year," I said as cheerfully as I could.

"Are you ever going to propose to me?" she asked, her voice scratchy and dry. It was a demand, not a question. She set down her empty glass.

I cleared my throat and tried to think of something to say.

"We talked about getting engaged a whole year ago!" she blurted out. I was glad she had put down the glass, or she might have thrown it through the cathedral window at the skiers.

"I told my family we'd announce our engagement by the end of the year. It didn't happen at Christmas dinner, or my dad's birthday party, or the New Year's Eve party. You sit on your hands like you're avoiding picking up a check. Not a word about a getting married. What's wrong with you? You're embarrassing me in front of my whole family."

I cleared my throat again. "I didn't think we agreed to be engaged by New Year's. We talked about it, but I don't remember anything specific. I heard you tell your mother that's what you expected."

"Well, ok, I did tell her, and she told everyone else. It's just that I thought you'd initiate something and surprise me and my family. But no, it didn't happen, and everyone's going home in a day or so. New Year's is almost over. Just skiing and dinners at the lodge."

Cheryl breezed down the stairs and into the living room, wearing a colorful robe with a wide belt and a New Year's nightcap that most of her hair fit under. No makeup yet, but her face looked freshly washed.

"Good morning, kids!"

Jenna barely turned her head. "Hi, Mom," she said joylessly.

"Hi, sweetheart. Happy New Year! Glad to see you're both up."

"Yes, Mother, we're here talking." Her mother gave her a peck on the cheek and a snatch of a hug.

"Oh, that's nice, a New Year's morning talk. That's wonderful," she said. "Your dad's already in the gym for his little workout, and I wanted to see if you two were joining us for brunch."

Jenna's mother turned toward me. "Hi, dear. Happy New Year from me and Gus," she said as I started to get up. She planted a kiss on my head and gave me a pat on the shoulder. "No, don't get up. You're reading your paper. I just wanted to see what you kids have planned this morning. Gus and I were hoping you'll make it for brunch. He has a table reserved looking over the ski lift."

"Sure, Mother, we'll be there," Jenna said. "Right, Dane?" Her glare said that if I didn't agree, I might as well pack my bags.

"Of course. I wouldn't miss it," I said, thankful for a group setting where the pressure wouldn't be as intense as being alone with Jenna. I knew things would deteriorate if we spent the morning in the condo alone.

"Wonderful!" her mother said. "We'll have a nice time before people start leaving. Your dad has the places set, and you're on both sides of us. We have the view of the ski lift. You'll love it."

The count at brunch was eighteen: Jenna's parents, brother and sister and their spouses and three kids. Her dad's brother, his wife, their three kids, and four grandkids. I had trouble with everyone's names and addressed them by name only when someone else mentioned it and I could repeat it. I was barely batting above .200 for the weekend, as Jenna always reminded me.

"They're my family now, but with any luck, they'll be yours one day, too. You should learn their names before."

She was right.

I was to sit next to her dad, a dark-haired, overweight, handsome Italian who'd made a fortune in retail and loved being a generous host and community booster. His name was Augustus, but everyone called him Gus. We had had pleasant but not long conversations in the two years I had dated Jenna. Gus was always working or socializing with his buddies at the Italian-American fraternal lodge or at charity and booster events. He was well-known and respected in town. He and his wife divided the family responsibilities evenly; Gus was the breadwinner and community activist while his wife, Cheryl, was the keeper of family traditions, hostess, and organizer of events like New Year's weekend.

Gus had already had a Bloody Mary or two by the time we arrived. His brother and his family were already seated across from Gus and me. Between the two brothers was a half-filled pitcher of tomato juice, vodka, and Tabasco sauce sitting next to a tray of celery sticks. When Gus had first spotted us coming across the room, he had grabbed the pitcher, poured a glass for me, and stuck in a celery stick. He stirred my drink and put it at my setting.

I reached down, gave Cheryl a kiss and hug from the back, and pulled out Jenna's chair. Cheryl was busy talking to her sister-in-law. Between them was a pitcher of mimosas that was half full. The sisters-in-law's conversation was accompanied by dynamic hand gestures to accent their loud and slightly drunken voices. I was almost afraid someone would get their eyes poked out by their fingers stabbing the air or by an errant sweep of arms laden with bracelets.

"How you doing, son?" Gus said, patting me on the arm as I sat down. "I fixed you a little eye-opener. I thought you might need it after last night. Great party, wasn't it?"

I took a well-deserved sip, grateful for a little hair of the dog. "It sure was, Gus. The band was great, and we all had a fabulous time. Best ever."

He reached down and patted me on the knee. "Glad you liked it. You're always welcome, you know that. Cheryl and I like you."

He went back to talking to his brother, standing to greet the rest of the family when they arrived. Waiters refilled water glasses as well as the Bloody Mary and mimosa pitchers around the table.

After everyone arrived, we got into a line at a buffet table loaded with steaming trays of eggs Benedict, scrambled eggs, huevos rancheros, sausage, bacon, ham, chicken breasts, crepes, French toast, waffles, and three kinds of potatoes. The next buffet table offered fruit bowls, Waldorf salad, bagels, toast, danishes, pitchers of fruit juices, milk, and coffee and tea dispensers. The only foods missing were baked beans and shish kebab.

By noon, Gus's guests were stuffed and pleasantly drunk. We weren't the largest or loudest table. Some people looked liked they had come right from the ballroom last night after a change of clothes, with no interruption of boisterous talking and drinking.

I hadn't had much of a chance to talk to Gus or his brother. Their conversation had been steady and included other family members. Gus had politely asked me about my new job and said that Jenna thought my apartment was "cute."

I felt tired from eating too much rich food and drinking too many Bloody Marys. I wanted to go back to the condo to take a nap and catch a bowl game or two. I was looking for Michigan in the Rose Bowl and Tennessee in the Orange Bowl. After two bowl games, I'd be ready for a nightcap and the sack. I was sure Jenna had other plans for the afternoon, and I was praying they didn't include me. I was also mature enough to acknowledge that all prayers aren't answered.

Without any lead-in, Gus started talking to me in a low tone without looking my way. "So you think you'll stay in Shattuck?"

I perked up. I wanted to stay on good terms with Gus, regardless of the deteriorating state of my relationship with his daughter. "I think so, Gus. The job looks promising, and I've found a couple neighborhoods that looking interesting. I'm considering buying a condo in the spring. I need to be a homeowner in that market."

He patted me on the back. "Good for you! And after that, see if you can pick up a duplex or small apartment as an investment. You can't go wrong owning real estate."

"I'll keep it in mind, Gus. Thanks for the tip."

"You need any help with the down payment?"

"No, I've got that covered, Gus. Thanks anyway. You're very kind."

He reached into his coat pocket and pulled out a cigar. I knew in a few minutes he'd head outside and fire it up. He loved cigars and had even gotten me puffing them occasionally. Back in the condo, I already had three that he had given me this weekend.

He rolled the cigar around in his fingers, aching to light up in the restaurant. "I got a feeling you and Jenna might not get married. None of my business; it's just a feeling I have."

He stuffed the cigar in his mouth, twirled it around, and took it out as if he had taken a puff.

"No hard feelings if it doesn't work out, son. I was engaged three times and had a flock of girlfriends before I popped the question to Cheryl. Best thing I ever did—get it out of my system and settle down after I'd gotten my wild oats sown. You don't look the wild oats kind of guy, but maybe you're not ready to get married and settle down for life. It's a big decision. Don't do it until all the signs are right and you feel it in your gut. You don't feel it in your gut, move on. Take my advice. And no matter what happens, you're a first-rate guy in my book, no matter what anyone else says. You need any help anytime, you know, to buy a duplex or a little apartment, just call me and I'll see what I can do."

"Sure thing, Gus. Thanks for the offer," I said as he pushed back his chair and stuck the cigar in his mouth. He was off to the deck to smoke it.

What a prince!

Chapter Eighteen

It was a hard March rain as I pulled up in front of Nancy's house on Cedar Lane near my old home in suburban Seattle.

Nancy's home looked comfortably familiar, the only change being taller fir trees in her front yard. They had grown at least a foot since the last time I was there three years ago. Nancy and I had team-taught a fourth-grade class at Lakeside Elementary School until my family was taken from me. I had dropped out of teaching soon after and had been on an extended leave of absence ever since.

I dashed up to Nancy's front door, shielding my head with a plastic cap. She opened the door without my knocking and I rushed in, rain water falling off me like a morning shower.

Nancy was home with her new baby, Melinda, who was born at Christmastime. While I took off my wet raincoat, Nancy put a finger to her lips. "Shhh, Melinda is sleeping. She's got colic and is cranky all the time. I don't think I'll ever sleep again."

I hung my raincoat on a hook alongside her family's dry raincoats and hats. Seattle, winter rain, wet clothes, soggy shoes: They are the reasons people love or hate it there.

Dry and coatless, I hugged Nancy, and she led me back through the living room into her kitchen.

"BJ, it's so wonderful to see you again. Everyone asks if I've talked to you and what you're doing. I was so happy you called. I can't wait to hear what you've been up to."

We sat down in the breakfast nook overlooking her backyard, where leafless apple and cherry trees lined the back fence. The backyard had a garden with cabbage and root vegetables in the winter. Between the fruit trees and the winter garden were her children's gym set and sandbox, emptied for the winter. I always liked her backyard. She and her neighbors shared a grove of towering spruce and fir trees as thick as a forest. It's lovely, and it always gives a sense of being remote while in a quaint suburb.

Nancy poured us coffee and brought over a plate of cookies and brownies left over from her oldest child's recent birthday party.

"So, please, tell me, what have you been doing and where have you been?" she said.

It felt good to be with Nancy again. We had shared so much when we taught and had become best friends, even though we hadn't spent much time together the last three years.

"Where do I start?" I began, feeling anxious about telling her. "This winter I've been mostly in Phoenix with my brother and his family. They had twin boys last fall and are knee-deep in diapers. Their little girl is just turning three. I help them by babysitting, giving them time to get away. I spent Christmas in Hawaii with girls from college. They live there and invited me to come anytime I'm on the West Coast. I spent last summer at our beach house, where I go every July. And that's about it."

"How exciting. Thanks for sending those cards. I love them. I take them to school and share with everyone. I've got them posted in the teachers' lounge so everyone can see them. Have you been by Lakeside to say hello?"

I smiled. "No, not yet. I wanted to come and see you first. I wanted to ask you if you're going back in the fall."

"Oh, yes, I have to. My maternity leave is up in June, and we need the money. My mother-in-law is going to help with Melinda part-time, and I'll get her in a babysitting service when she can't make it. I actually miss the kids at school, if you can believe that. Changing diapers for one is not the same as herding a classroom of eight-year-olds. That's actually easier, as you know."

"I'm glad to hear you're going back. That's what I want to talk to you about. I'm thinking about coming back next year."

She squealed. "Really! Oh, that would be so great, BJ. That makes me really happy."

"How would you like to work as a team again?"

"Perfect! If I have anything to say about it, we will. Have you told anyone else? Have you spoken to Mr. Higgins?"

I shook my head. "Not yet, but I'm going tomorrow. I called his secretary and asked for an appointment. He called back an hour later and said if I was coming back to work, he'd see me tomorrow at 10:00 a.m."

"You're a shoo-in, BJ. He asks about you all the time and tells me you can have your old job back anytime. Everyone will be thrilled. Do you think you're ready to come back?"

I nodded. "This time I am. I thought about it last spring, but it was too early. I was still a little . . . shaky . . . and didn't think I could handle the pressure after just two years off. But this spring, I am getting excited thinking about getting in the classroom and doing what I love best."

"All it takes is time," Nancy said, reaching over to squeeze my hand. "You've got so many friends here, and all the teachers are behind you one hundred percent. I know they'll help if you think the time is right. And you look great! You've put on a little weight; I can see it in your face. And you look happy."

I was pleased she noticed. The last time I had seen Nancy, I was still recovering from my losses and had lost too much weight.

"Thanks. I do feel so much better. It was hard the first couple years. To be honest, I didn't know if I could make it. But with counseling, spending time with friends, and taking care of myself, I'm starting to feel like my old self again. And part of that is because of last summer."

"Tell me, what happened?"

I smiled. "It's so funny . . . and almost like a soap opera. You know, I've always spent July at our beach house on the East Coast. Well, one day last summer, I bumped into this nice man at a coffee house, and we spent several wonderful, happy days together."

Nancy grinned and put her hands out toward me. "Tell me! I can't wait to hear!"

"Like I said, it sounds almost silly. We met one morning at a coffee shop when he bumped me and spilled my iced tea on my arm. He apologized, wiped it off, and was like a little kid who had broken a Christmas ornament. He was so embarrassed that he blushed. So I invited him to sit down, and he brought me another iced tea, and we started talking.

Nothing special, just easy chatter about being at the beach. He seemed so friendly and genuine. On the spur of the moment, I invited him to the beach house to swim. He came over; we swam all afternoon, and had lunch. It just felt right, being with him. I haven't really dated in a long time. So the next day I invited him to go sailing, and we had another fun day. We went biking the day after that, and the poor guy tipped over and sprained his ankle. I took him to the hospital, and after he was bandaged up, I took him back to the house and nursed him for another day."

Nancy was smiling, "And, was there any . . . ?"

I winked. "I knew you'd ask. You'd never let me go about that. Well, a little . . . hugging, smooching . . . and yes, we did sleep together. I hadn't slept with a man since the accident. I was sort of shocked that the first time I did was with a man I had just met. I can't believe how fast things developed. It was almost scary . . . but it also felt right."

"So, what's his name? Where does he live? When did you see him last? When are you going to see him again?"

I laughed and held up my hand. "Ok, one at a time. His name is Dane. He works in Shattuck up the coast a few hours, and for the life of me, all I know is that he does consulting. No idea what that means, really. I haven't seen him since July, but we're getting together this July at the beach house."

"You haven't seen him since July?" Nancy said, looking puzzled. "How often have you talked?"

I shook my head. "We haven't. I told him I had a busy year ahead and would like to have some time away."

"Hmm, that might be a little hard for a guy. I'm sure he likes you and would like to keep in touch."

"I'm sure he would. But to be honest, I wanted time alone to work out things. If we were talking long distance a lot, it would feel like pressure. And I don't want that now."

Nancy looked at me, and I could tell something was going on in her head. I hadn't told anyone else about Dane, but he had been on my mind every day. I had even dreamed about him, about our times at the beach. Some of the dreams were surrealistic with no connection to real places or events. I'd have to ask my old Seattle therapist about the dreams. I was glad I'd made an appointment to see her next week while I was in town.

"I guess you just have to decide those things in your own time frame. Do you miss him?"

I nodded. "Yes, and I'm looking forward to seeing him in July."

"Good. That's a very good sign. And when do we get to meet him?"

I laughed. "In time, in time. Let's get through this summer, and I'll tell you how it went in the fall."

"I've got a feeling, BJ," she said, a grin on her face. "A good one. You haven't seemed this alive and connected since . . . the accident."

"I didn't think I could ever have these feelings again. But they're coming back."

Chapter Nineteen

I parked where BJ used to park, in front of the dune closest to the back entrance of her beach house. I was nervous: palms sweating, heart racing. *What am I doing here?* It was only May; I wasn't going to see BJ until July. Yet something was pulling me back to her beach house. She wouldn't be here, but I had to return, go in, and see if the house was the way I remembered it. I hadn't been able to get BJ or her beach house out of my mind in ten months. I just had to see if it was real.

I reached into my pocket, where I kept the purloined key. That's what I had called it ever since it had dropped out of my shirt. Right after BJ had come out of the guest bedroom that last morning, we had started talking. Our conversation had been so intense that I couldn't concentrate on anything but what she was saying. I had forgotten all about the key in my pocket until I got to the motel that night.

Three things from our last conversation kept playing over in my memory.

"This has been a wonderful few days, Dane. I can't thank you enough for rescuing me from a week alone at the beach house."

I wasn't sure what rescue meant, but she had smiled when she said it. It could have been flirtatious—or something more intimate than that.

"If you like, I'd like to meet you again here next summer. I'll be away the rest of the year visiting family and friends."

I was a little puzzled by this. She hadn't indicated if she worked or how she supported herself. I had purposely kept questions from veering into personal details. The signal I got from her was she wanted to keep her privacy, at least in the early stages of our relationship. *Is four days together almost night and day a relationship? Or just an acquaintance?* I certainly wanted a relationship with her.

"I need time to myself before we get together, so I hope you'll understand if I ask that we don't keep in touch with phone calls or letters."

That set me back. Why not keep in touch, even an occasional phone call or letter? But I wanted to respect her request. I had the sense that she felt she had confided too much the previous night and wanted to back away from getting too close too soon. I had never had that experience myself, getting so close in such a short time with anyone. I promised her I wouldn't call; in fact, I didn't even have her phone number and hadn't asked for it.

But she had never been out of my mind since our last day together.

I reflected back on that day. It had been muggy and hot, ninety-four degrees. The air conditioning had been blasting in my car as I had driven off—with a mist in my eyes. I had felt so overcome by my emotions. For days afterward, I had been unable to really concentrate on anything but BJ. I had driven to Shattuck, checked into a motel, and gone to my interview. I had started my new job in a fog that didn't lift for weeks.

My purloined key fit in the back door, and I went into the garage. It looked as familiar as the day I had left: the small sailboat on a trailer with its mast down in one bay; kayaks, canoes, bass boat in the other bay; and tackle boxes, creels, rods and reels, swim masks, and snorkels on shelves along the wall.

I opened the door to the main house and was surprised at how dark it was. Curtains had been drawn over the sliding glass doors facing the beach. The doors to the upstairs bedrooms were open but little light came from them. Curtains were probably pulled there also to keep out the sun and prying eyes.

My heart was beating faster as I moved quietly into the dining area and living room. The sofa still faced out like it had our last day together. I went over to the hutch where BJ had put the extra keys. I opened the top drawer, and there they were in a lacquer box along with coins, medallions, and tchotchkes. I picked up two silver keys that matched mine. I don't know why, but I was intrigued by the keys. BJ had mentioned giving two keys to caretakers. She had her own key, and there were these two spares—and my purloined key. Six keys to the beach house.

I walked to the sliding glass doors and pulled back the curtain. Sunlight slashed into the room, brightening the middle of the house. I closed it and walked past the entertainment center with the TV and stereo. Interesting, we had never turned on the TV the entire time we were together last July. BJ had played a couple of CDs of symphonies, reggae, and cello. But most of the time we had been too absorbed in each other to pay attention to music.

I went into the kitchen and opened the refrigerator door. A couple of bottles of wine, sodas, juices, and jams. I looked in cabinets but found only boxes of cereal, rice, pasta, cans of vegetables, and tins of teas and coffees. Other cabinets held plates and cups that were familiar from our meals there.

I walked into the guest bedroom, where we had spent our last night together. This was where I had heard her story, where we had made love, and where we had showered in the morning. That night had been seared in my memory, hearing her tragic story of losing her family in the car accident.

I went into the bathroom and turned on the light. I ran a hand over the double-sink counter where I had shaved that last morning and where she had put on makeup and combed her hair. She had teased me as she watched me shave while I kept looking at her naked body in the mirror. She had called me a dirty old man before punching me in the arm and sticking out her tongue at me. Three hours later, I had driven away from her house.

The bed was made with the same covers. Extra pillows were thrown against the headboard. The curtains were closed. I looked in the closet for the first time. It was crowded with men's and women's shirts, pants, beachwear, casual shoes, and slippers. No dress wear or suits or coats. The top shelf was lined with baseball caps and floppy hats appropriate for the beach, along with boxes I didn't open. A half dozen umbrellas stood in the corner.

The last places to visit were BJ's bedroom and the study upstairs. Although I had been in the study only twice to select books, it was the one room I wanted to spend more time in and explore. I climbed the steps slowly, remembering our hours in her bedroom. I was having unusual feelings of something like voyeurism or obsession to enter her bedroom alone without her knowing.

I headed to the study first and walked in reverently. The room was dark; the single window behind the leather chair and desk was covered by a heavy curtain. I didn't want to spoil the effect by turning on a light, so I let my eyes get used to the dark. I walked over to the bookcase, running my hand over the titles, reading the larger ones in the faint light. I passed in front of the desk, put my hand on the globe, and went to the other side, where the fiction, histories, and biographies were shelved. One could spend years here, reading the classics and histories—getting a classical education without stepping into a classroom. And in the most serene setting I could imagine, at the beach with BJ, enjoying time to ourselves and indulging our tastes in reading, music, arts, entertaining, and each other. *A wonderful fantasy.*

I was getting ahead of things, projecting too much into what we had so far. But it was delightful to imagine reading these books with BJ, with no end to our time together.

I went back to the hall looking over the main house and headed to BJ's bedroom. This was the room I felt the most anxiety about. Here she had slept, made love, and had many intimate memories.

The room was dark, the shades pulled on the north and east sides facing the beach. Her bed was covered in the same yellow and blue cover with extra pillows. A blanket was folded at the foot.

I peeked out the shades to look down on the beach. Not a soul to be seen to the north and only a few in the distance toward town. I went back and sat on the edge of her bed. A Bible, three paperbacks, a disconnected clock, and a picture of her family were on her nightstand. I picked up the photograph and looked at the faces. BJ looked to be about twenty-eight, her hair long and flowing, holding Sylvia in her arms when she was about three. I felt sad and lonely, like I had most months since we had been together. This was the first picture I had seen of her since July.

I went over to the wall where she kept her photo gallery of family, friends, vacations, and beach time. The top row was ancestors in formal poses at weddings or family reunions along with studio portraits, all in black and white. The middle row was BJ's family and parents during holidays and at the beach. I felt strange again, looking at her secretly as if I were spying. But I couldn't help myself; I needed a connection to BJ, even if it meant stealing into her house and reliving cherished memories from last July.

I went back downstairs and sat on the sofa with the shade open just enough to see the surf.

In two months I would come back to BJ, and we would hopefully pick up where we had left things last July.

What had she done this past year? Having no contact was unsettling. I thought about her every day and replayed our conversations over and over. So many times I had wanted to hear her soft voice and her throaty laugh and tell her how much I missed her and couldn't wait to reconnect.

How had the last ten months been for her? Had she thought about our four days last July with the same affection and hope that I had?

Fifty-four days until I would come back. This time would be different. I hoped it would be way different. I hoped we would never leave each other again.

Chapter Twenty

I opened the back door, and there he was, head turned to the side with a sly grin, sunglasses on his head, wearing his red and white bathing suit and T-shirt, ready for the beach.

"First Mate Chambers, returning for summer duty," he said, his voice breaking. He made a mock salute, his palm at his forehead.

His goofy gesture was sweet. "All hands present," I answered, returning his salute. "The crew's waiting." I was thrilled to see him.

I had been nervous about our reunion, but the butterflies flew away as soon as we hugged and I felt the warmth of his embrace. It felt so good to have him in my arms again. My heart was racing like a greyhound.

We kissed and I never wanted to let him go. After we broke, I leaned back to take a long look at him.

"Wow, that was great kiss, Cap'n!" he said. "Can we do that again?"

We laughed and hugged again. The ice was broken.

"Come in before we scare the seagulls," I said, taking his hand and leading him into the house. "I've got lunch ready, and we can head to the beach. How was your drive?"

He entered the garage, and I watched him looking over that boats and beach gear. He had seemed fascinated by the boats and fishing gear before, and it still captured his attention. I meant to ask him about that sometime.

"I was counting the minutes until I got here," said Dane. "That last hour was torture."

"Do you have anything in the car you need to bring in?"

"Just a few clothes and books. Nothing important."

"Bring them in; I've got the guest room ready for you." I had wanted to start slowly and see how things progressed. But after our greeting kiss and hugs, I felt confident our days ahead would be as memorable as last year. It was good to have him here again.

"I'll get them later. I want to see you and the house. I've thought about this place many times."

We walked through the garage, arms around each other's waist. I couldn't believe how natural it seemed to be touching him. It had been a long year, but we were together again. It seemed like we had never parted. But I reminded myself to take things slowly until we got used to each other once more.

We walked hand in hand into the house, and I led him to the front. I had opened the sliding glass doors a few inches, and a gentle breeze was coming from the beach.

"There's our beach, waiting for us," I said. "I've got towels, goggles, and snorkel in case you want to swim after lunch."

"You bet. I've been working out all winter to get ready for your summer beach Olympics."

"Let's have a bite to eat before we go out. Are you hungry?"

He nodded. "I could use something. I only had coffee and a bagel for breakfast."

I took him into the kitchen, where I had set trays, glasses, and an ice bucket ready to go out onto the patio. I took out cucumber sandwiches, salad, sliced cheeses, cold cuts, and antipasto I had fixed last night from the refrigerator.

"What would you like to drink? I've got beer, wine, soft drinks, water, and iced tea."

"Iced tea would be perfect."

"Get the pitcher out of the fridge and pour two glasses for us. I'll meet you outside."

I took the trays and went out to the patio, where I had set places with linen, silverware, cups, and plates. I set out food out and waited for him. He brought the glasses and pitcher of iced tea.

Before we started to eat, I reached over and squeezed his hand. "It's so nice to see you again, Dane. I've missed you."

A warm smile came over his face, his soft brown eyes sparkling.

"I've thought about you every day and remembered our four days together. It was a very special time. Four days that went by fast but lasted a year."

"Four days. Is that all it was? I thought we were together almost a week," I said.

We started to eat, munching on sandwiches and forking cheese, olives, and antipasto onto our plates.

"Tuesday we went swimming, Wednesday sailing, Thursday biking, and I left Friday afternoon."

"It seemed longer than four days. The time went fast, but we did so much and got to know each other. Four days. It's amazing what happened in that time."

"Yes, it was."

"I hope we have more time this summer. I have a week's vacation."

"Great! I have a week or even longer, if I need it."

We ate quickly, chatting about little details from the year apart but not opening up to any real personal information. After lunch, we took the dishes in, stacked them in the sink, and headed right to the beach.

We put our towels down in the same place as last year. Dane was about to sit down when I slapped him on the rear and said, "Last one in the water has to make dinner!" I dashed toward the waves.

He was a step or two behind me, but as I dove into the surf, he was alongside me. We went through one wave, surfaced behind it, cheered, and dove into the next wave that crashed over us.

When the wave had moved past us, we came up inches from each other and fell into each other's arms. We kissed, clinging to each other until the next wave knocked us over. We were sent cascading toward the shore, our bodies entwined, rolling underwater, hanging on to each other until we spilled onto the beach, coughing and spitting out water. Splayed awkwardly on the sand like beached seals, we lunged for each other, held on tight, and fell back on the sand in a passionate embrace.

Chapter Twenty-One

The sailboat sliced through the waves as we pushed off from shore at the Otter Creek marina and headed into the ship channel. BJ was at the wheel, I was running the lines, and we were headed to open ocean for another glorious day at sea.

BJ had prepared everything for sailing, from getting the sailboat ready to packing lunch and snorkeling gear and planning a new adventure she was keeping secret. The sailboat was on the trailer and hitched to a truck, all ready for us when we arrived at the yard that morning. The boatyard crew was waiting for us and teased BJ as she introduced me again. She grabbed a camera from her purse, handed it to one of them, and moved us behind the stern to get a picture with *Young, Lucky and In Love* behind us.

The crew joked and teased as we climbed into the truck hauling the boat and headed to the gate on our way to Otter Creek. Secretly, I think BJ enjoyed the teasing and jousting from the guys.

The tide was in our favor as we reached open waters a couple of hundred yards off shore. BJ had told me we were going someplace new, southeast about thirty miles offshore, but she wouldn't tell me what we would find there. She said I'd like it and would get a taste of history.

"Think nautical archeology," she said after I persisted with more questions. "Let's just say that you'll see something today that you've never seen before and may never see again in your life."

"Where is it?" I asked, realizing it was a dumb question as soon as it came out of my mouth.

"Out there," she pointed east, where all I could see was the ocean. "Ten miles out, there's an upraised sand bank where the continental shelf drops two thousand feet to the bottom of the ocean. We're going right to the edge. Fall off, and you'll end up in silt where worms scavenge flesh off dead whales. It's so cold your blood will freeze."

Her image was so graphic my heart skipped a beat.

I was quiet as we sailed east, visualizing BJ's description of the bottom of the ocean. She enjoyed shocking me. It wasn't an experience I was familiar with, but I found myself stimulated by the way she seemed to be taking us to the edge, so to speak.

BJ looked impressive at the helm; assured, calm, focused. She paid attention to the wind and currents, checking charts and listening to the marine channel. She sent me below for marine binoculars and then scanned the horizon like she knew what she was looking for. I sat on the gunwale, look-ing at the clouds, seabirds, disappearing coastline, and open ocean. Wherever I looked, there were spectacular views. I was transfixed, trying to take in the experience with all my senses as BJ navigated us far from land.

The sun was hot and relentless. I wore a cap, sunblock, sunglasses, and a long-sleeved shirt to protect against the strong rays of the July sun. We consumed drinks from the cooler one after the other. I dipped my hands over the side to wipe cold water over my skin.

An hour out, I saw something on the horizon. One object, then a second. Two boats bobbing in the waves. BJ trained her binoculars on them and made a small course correction to put us on line to reach them. She navigated us toward them and got on the marine channel to announce our imminent arrival.

They responded, and we moved closer. We sailed around them and then tacked to the lee side. Fifty yards from them, BJ threw over water anchors and waved at the crew on the boats. They yelled out with a bullhorn.

"Ahoy! We're diving below. Have a team inspecting the Nazi submarine. Are you going to dive?"

BJ yelled across, "No, we're just here to observe. We'll snorkel topside and watch what you're doing. Just nosy tourists."

BJ went below for snorkels, goggles, and life preservers. "We're not at Gull Point anymore. We're in open ocean. Wear a life preserver anytime you go in the water."

I tossed my hat, sunglasses, and shirt below and put on the life preserver, goggles, and mask. I sat on the gunwale waiting for BJ.

She fell over backward in a cascade of bubbles and disappeared. I followed. When I surfaced, I blew water out of my snorkel and searched around. She was paddling toward the boats, her head underwater. I followed, uneasy about the deep blue water below that seemed endless. I couldn't see bottom; it was an alarming sensation.

The water was cold and choppy, rolling over me as I swam toward BJ. The waves were a couple of feet high and relentless. I adjusted to the constant rolling motion as I made my way forward. This was more challenging than Gull Point. And dangerous!

I had never swum in the open ocean before, only at beaches, where the sloping sand below was reassuring if I wanted to reach down and touch my toes below water.

Following BJ for a minute or so, I saw a faint glow of light below. The glow became two lights. I swam farther and saw small figures swimming lazily, bubbles rising from their scuba gear: three divers in black wetsuits, swimming over a bulky object the size of a school bus. As I got closer, I saw the outline of a boat, the bow and stern covered in seaweed and sand. The closer I looked, the more I could see; it wasn't the size of a school bus but as large as a railroad car.

It took shape. I could see the outline of a Nazi submarine. A chill ran over me as I realized what I was looking at: wreckage from World War II that had been lying on the bottom of the Atlantic ten miles from shore.

The divers swam over the wreckage, shining torches over the hull, moving along the sides, hovering above circles that must have been hatches. One diver motioned to another and then disappeared down one of the open hatches.

I watched in shock. How dangerous! I shivered as I imagined how many things could go wrong in the darkness below deck.

A second diver followed the first down the hatch. All that remained was bubbles rising from the open hatch. The bubbles stopped, then resumed as a ribbon of smaller bubbles rising from the deck. The divers were moving through the sub, bow to stern. They were below deck for a couple of minutes, tiny bubbles rising as they swam toward the stern.

Then one diver, followed by the other, swam out from the stern, their light appearing and larger bubbles rising. I was relieved.

I bumped into BJ, her fins hitting the top of my head. She turned, faced me, her mask covering all but her eyes. I could tell she was smiling. She poked her thumb up and down to express her excitement. I reached out to squeeze her hand.

I was madly in love with this wild, adventurous woman! Being with BJ was the most exciting experience I had ever had. What was next?

Chapter Twenty-Two

"I've got something special planned for us today," BJ said as we toweled off the next morning after showering. She had a twinkle in her eye that told me she was really looking forward to the day.

"I'll follow you all the way to Africa," I said, drying my hair as we eyed each other in the mirror of her double-sink bathroom, still naked from our showers. "Or to Antarctica or the Himalayas. Just tell me where, and I'll be on the first plane with you."

"How about boating up the Amazon?" she asked.

"Oooh, I think I might hold back there. They've got piranhas in the Amazon, and they chew up people who fall off boats. I've never wanted to be fish bait."

"I've found your limit. Fish bait is out." She grinned as she hung up her towel.

Then she turned and looked into my eyes with more seriousness, our light banter temporarily behind us. "It is so . . . refreshing to enjoy your spirit, Dane. I've never found anyone who liked spontaneous adventure so much. In fact, I hadn't thought that *I* was this adventurous a person, but something about you makes me want to try things I haven't done before." She took both of my hands in hers, standing naked before me and looking like an Egyptian goddess. "It is such *fun* to find someone who will accept any challenge I put out."

She kissed me tenderly on the lips, then let go of my hands and turned back to the mirror. "Anyway, don't get your hopes up," she continued, resuming her previous teasing tone. "Today won't be adventurous. Just fun and relaxing. We're going to the farmers market to stock up on fresh vegetables and fruits. I go every week and love picking up the fresh fruit. They've got music and crafts, corn dogs, kettle corn, barbecue, fried okra, biscuits, and buttered beans to die for. You'll love it."

"Adventures in eating, that sounds like fun," I said. "I thought you were going to propose we go parachuting out of a plane or spelunking in caves." I reached over to poke BJ in the ribs. She flinched, poked me back, and then fell into my arms and kissed me.

I put my arms around her waist and walked us into her bedroom in full embrace, balancing to keep us close together without tripping. We fell back on BJ's unmade bed with her on top of me.

After tea, fruit, and scrambled eggs, we headed out the backdoor to BJ's car. She had a colorful beach bag for shopping and wore large sunglasses, a wide-brimmed beach hat with a red and blue band around the brim, a gauzy top, a wraparound skirt with a slit up the side, and stylish sandals that showed her red toenails. She was as fetching and seductive as a Hollywood actress. I was crazy in love with this woman.

We chattered like teenagers as she drove into town. We parked near the town center, which was lined with spruce and pine trees in front of the old courthouse. The courtyard was crowded with produce trucks and tented tables where vendors displayed vegetables and fruits stacked in mounds or wooden boxes with handwritten price tags.

BJ and I walked hand in hand down the rows, sampling fresh strawberries, cherry tomatoes, peaches, nectarines, and plums. Under one tent a vendor had trays of California olives, grapes, melons, and avocados. Other tents had baked goods of all varieties, including olive, garlic, and cheese breads, as well as cookies, cakes, muffins, rolls, tortillas, sourdough, and baguettes.

A bluegrass band wearing flannel shirts and coveralls was playing frisky tunes in the center courtyard while little children danced joyfully. Two young women painted kids' faces with flags, butterflies, smiley faces, and cartoon characters. Another woman wearing a multicolored balloon hat and clown face twisted balloons into animal figures and crazy hats for kids. A circle of children surrounded another vendor who was handing out plastic toys that emitted trails of bubbles when swirled around.

Retired couples strolled about the lawn, pushing carriages of grandchildren. Groups of adolescents and teenagers snaked through the crowd wearing T-shirts of their schools or favorite rock bands. Circles of young mothers cradled diapered babies and chattered about their families. Dads wearing baseball caps and shirts of sports teams sipped beer from cups and smoked cigars. Politicians wearing name badges were handing out buttons, kissing babies, shaking hands, and laughing too hard.

I followed behind BJ as she filled her beach bag with assorted delights from the vendors. We were in line at a bread stall when I heard a deep Southern drawl above the noise of the crowd and banjo music.

"Well, look who's here. BJ, buying up the whole place."

A tall, distinguished-looking gentleman with white hair came toward us, his sunburned face beaming at BJ.

A smile spread over BJ's face, and she hugged the older man. "Oh, Simms, it's wonderful to see you. Is Mattie here?"

"She's right here," he said, his drawl thick as maple syrup.

From behind the tall man came a white-haired woman wearing a pink summer dress and carrying an oversized straw purse in red, blue, green, yellow, and orange.

"BJ, don't you look darling in that pretty outfit," she said, giving BJ a peck on the cheek. Her drawl was slightly less syrupy.

"It's so nice to see both of you. I've been meaning to come over," BJ said.

"Well, what about tonight, dear?" Mattie said. "We're having a party for Bob and his family. They're here from Atlanta with our new granddaughter. We're having a barbecue for a few friends to show off the pretty little thing, and we'd love to have you come by."

"Well, thank you, Mattie. Could I bring a friend?" she said, reaching over to pull me closer. "This is Dane. We've been at the beach house, and I'm showing him around the farmers market. Dane, this is Simms Russell and his wife, Mattie. They've been special friends of my parents for as long as I can remember."

"How do you do, son," Simms said, giving my hand a vigorous pump. "Any friend of BJ's is a friend of ours. We'd love to have you come over and meet our friends if it's not too much trouble."

"I'm sure we'd enjoy it, sir. But I'll have to wait until BJ invites me," I said.

Mattie winked at BJ and said, "BJ, I hope you don't take too long to bring this nice young man over. It's nice you're showing him around. Our farmers market is one of the best things about our town in the summer. I love it here. So many nice families enjoying themselves and buying healthy food that our farmers bring us. They're the bedrock of our little community."

"What time? And can we bring something?" BJ asked.

"Don't bring a thing, dear," Mattie said, swatting at the air as if to shoo away bugs. "We're having drinks at six-thirty and barbecue at seven-thirty. Please come for the cocktail hour; many people you know will be there. They'll be so happy to hear you're back in town for the summer."

Chapter Twenty-Three

We swam, read, and relaxed on the beach after the farmers market. It was a quiet day for us, but we felt so comfortable together that we didn't have to chatter like we had the first couple of days. Our conversations had become casual and easy, sharing whatever popped into our minds.

BJ gave me a briefing as we drove to the Russells that evening. As she spoke, I quietly admired how she looked. She wore a colorful Guatemalan dress and a bow in her hair, which she had teased into short curls.

The Russells were a very important family in town. When their children were small, they had moved from New York, where Simms had been an attorney for an international energy company. He had wanted to come back to Cabot's Harbor, where he had been raised, to raise their children in a small community. Their kids had gone on to excellent schools and were now raising young families themselves. The youngest son, Bob, had two kids and was the CFO of an agricultural equipment manufacturer. Barbara, BJ's friend from her teenage years, was the mother of three and owned a chain of health spas in Florida. Simms Jr., the oldest, was the state attorney general and eyeing the governor's seat for the next election.

Simms had started his own law firm when he returned to Cabot's Harbor and was semi-retired, having turned the firm over to a junior partner so he could spend more time at the country club, serving on the board of several nonprofits, and hosting parties at their spacious house on the eighteenth green of the country club. Simms had been BJ's father's attorney and close friend. They had golfed, fished, and advised aspiring local politicians and businessmen.

When BJ was growing up, she and Barbara had spent summers together at the beach. Barbara had introduced BJ to her friends, and they had attended sports events, parties, and dinners when BJ was in town. BJ said it was a little like attending two high schools, having close friends at the beach as well as her high school friends in Colorado.

We arrived at the country club, which was on a ridge overlooking the ocean and surrounded by a pine forest. BJ waved at the uniformed attendant who came out of the gatehouse. We drove through a grove of pines and passed alongside a fairway on a cliff overlooking the ocean. We followed the fairway to the green and a tee box, and then followed another long fairway cutting through the trees. In the distance I could see the clubhouse, with tennis courts on one side and a pool on the other.

The parking lot was filled with Cadilacs, Mercedes, Lexus, Acuras, Porsches, Jaguars, and a white Rolls-Royce at a spot marked for *President of Ocean View*. We drove through the parking lot, and it became a long lane lined with cypress trees along the eighteenth fairway, dog-legging to the left. A foursome in colorful pants and wide-brimmed hats was walking the course, followed by caddies and carts. Another foursome was waiting to tee up, shielding their eyes from the setting sun. The fairways were so green they looked painted. The sky was deep blue and cloudless. The parallel row of cypress trees was perfectly symmetrical and the same height. The trees stopped at a curve that took us onto a lane of sprawling homes on the eighteenth fairway.

The one-lane road was filled with cars of the same style and vintage as those in the parking lot. We parked and walked past landscaped homes of modern design, two-story townhouses with the second floor overlooking the fairways, and a larger ranch-style house on the fairway. Low bushes separated the fairways and homes. Residents could enjoy cocktails on their patios and watch golfers on their way down the fairways.

A black butler opened the door as we came up the winding brick walkway to the Russell home. He bowed, greeted us, and directed us through the dining room to the outdoor patio where people were drinking and eating appetizers around a kidney-shaped pool.

As soon as we stepped out on the patio, another butler handed us a tray of white and red wines. We both took white wine, and another waiter appeared, holding a tray of shrimp. We each took one, dipped them in cocktail sauce, and popped them in our mouths. I took another, but BJ moved off toward the pool.

"BJ, I'm so thrilled you came!" said a young, attractive woman, grabbing her in a full embrace. "Mom and Dad said they saw you at the market today. It's been ages since I've seen you." Both women squealed and hugged.

The woman spotted me over BJ's shoulder. "This must be that handsome man Mom was raving about. He *is* good-looking!"

"Barbara, this is Dane, my friend from Shattuck. We met last year, and he came down to spend a few days at our beach house."

Barbara reached for my hand and shook it warmly. "Dane, so wonderful to meet you. Mom was so impressed with you this afternoon. If you're with BJ, you've got to be a very lucky guy. She always had exquisite taste in men. Just ask my Clint. The first time I introduced him to BJ, I thought I'd never get his attention again."

The girls laughed and hugged again. "Come, I want you to see my kids. It's been forever since you saw them. They're growing like weeds."

Off they went, weaving through the crowds around the pool and the tables between the tennis courts and the brick barbecue, where white-capped chefs and assistants tended to a pig and a lamb roasting over pits. A buffet table covered in checkered tablecloths was set between the pool and barbecue. The table was filled with platters of sliced vegetables, salads, pastas, fresh corn, and potatoes. Two open bars at opposite ends of the pool were surrounded by older gentlemen in golf shirts, blazers, and freshly pressed slacks sipping martinis and wine.

I followed BJ most of the evening as people greeted her. She pulled me over to meet friends, spouses, and children, accompanied by much laughing and happy chatter. The sun was getting lower in the sky, and the air was cooling, turning it into a perfect evening for an outdoor summer party. Alcohol flowed freely, and everyone was on their best behavior, slapping backs, kissing cheeks, and not having a serious conversation about anything.

Mattie spotted me as folks were lining up at the buffet table, loading their plates while juggling their drinks.

She walked up and shook my hand. "Dane, I'm thrilled you came tonight. It's nice to see you with BJ. I haven't seen her happy in years. Everyone is so glad to see her; it's been awhile since she's been out. Whatever you're doing, I hope you don't quit. She needs a good man to show her how to live again. Be good to her and give her the love she needs."

Chapter Twenty-Four

The next couple of days were like the dog days of summer. The weather turned hotter and more humid, so we limited our time on the beach. We took drives along the shore, went to a matinee, and lunched in Cabot's Harbor. We walked around the town, the college, the parks, the neighborhoods, and the museum, which had artifacts and interpretive displays of the town's history back to the eighteenth century. Dane commented that he was feeling more like a resident than a tourist, and he could see why I had such affection for Cabot's Harbor. He said the Russells had a lot to be proud of, and he understood why they had returned from New York to raise their kids here and give them a solid sense of community.

In the mornings, we'd head onto the beach before the sun baked us like briskets. Sticky and sweating, we'd drag ourselves inside to sip cold drinks, nibble on fruit, and lie on the sofa in the air conditioning. We watched old movies on TV. Dane preferred Humphrey Bogart in *The African Queen* and *The Caine Mutiny*; my choices were Liza Minnelli in *Cabaret* and Cary Grant in *North by Northwest* and *Suspicion*.

If we didn't watch movies, we'd play favorite CDs, mine being John Coltrane, Miles Davis, k. d. lang, and Judy Collins. Dane liked show tunes—South Pacific, Music Man—and late '50s and '60s legends such as Buddy Holly, Jefferson Airplane, the Doors, and the Byrds. We'd snuggle on the sofa, nibble snacks, sip wine, and tease each other about musical and movie tastes. We'd get naked and fool around.

Dane asked a million questions about the people at the Russell's party. I told him stories about them and how I had met them, their families, and how often we had gotten together. I told him I hadn't been to Cabot's Harbor as much as I had in my teens and twenties, and I missed their sense of community and connectedness to each other.

I had traveled more than most of the local people, but I never bragged about it. Dad was on the road for long stretches, and we'd visit him in Europe, New York, or California when he'd be assigned somewhere for a couple months. Our family had been pretty mobile. After I went to college and married, I didn't return to the beach house as often as I had when I was younger. I was enjoying the connection again and told Dane I'd probably come every summer now.

"Who knows? I might even move here permanently if I remarry and settle down to raise a family."

Dane perked up when I mentioned this. "When do you think you might be ready to do that?"

I shrugged. "I don't know. I'm not ready now, but maybe in a year or two. I have a couple more things to do first."

"Such as?" he asked, leaning up on his elbow as we lay naked in the afternoon after watching *The Thomas Crown Affair.*

I paused, not wanting to reveal that this conversation was

taking me into areas that I wasn't comfortable confiding yet. It was still too early.

"I . . . I'm going back to teaching this fall," I said, letting out a long breath. It didn't sound like a difficult statement, but I got it out, the first time since I'd been with Nancy. I had been debating how I would tell Dane about my decision, knowing the topic could veer off in areas I still wanted to keep private.

He looked puzzled. "Where will you teach?"

"Back at my old elementary school outside Seattle. I went to see the principal last spring, and he offered the job to me. I'll be with my old team teacher again, and we'll have a fourth-grade class. They're my favorite group."

"When will you start?"

I was getting nervous and noticed myself wanting to get up and put my clothes on. I sat up and turned my back to Dane, grabbing the shirt I had been wearing. I got off the sofa, put it on, and headed toward the stairs. "I think I'll take a shower before we go back on the beach. Want to join me?"

He looked at me, and I could see he was disappointed. I left him on the sofa with only a towel covering him. He reached for his shorts and followed me up and into the bathroom. I turned on the shower and got in, keeping the water cool. I anticipated him reacting with frustration that I had left the sofa, where we had been snuggling comfortably. My departure had been abrupt, and I hoped he wasn't going to be angry that I had broken the mood. He got in the shower next to me without saying anything. I stood on my toes to give him a quick kiss on the lips.

"I start the third week in August. I go back for orientation and classroom preparation in a couple weeks. I'm a little nervous, to be honest. It's been almost four years since I was in the classroom."

There it was; I was going on and didn't want to get into details. He started with questions, and all I wanted to do was get out of the shower, slip into my bikini, go to the beach, and dive in the ocean. Enough personal stuff for one day.

"Which school?" he started. "Where will you live? I didn't know it was four years since you taught. Didn't you work after you left that job? How long will you teach? Did you think of teaching here?"

He was being kind and interested, but I couldn't get into answering all his questions now. I was out of the shower in a minute. I went into my bedroom and put on my bikini and grabbed a towel while Dane was still in the shower.

"I'll see you on the beach," I said as I headed for the stairs. "Bring a towel and a couple drinks when you come. It's blazing out there."

I was in tears as I ran onto the beach, leaving Dane behind in the shower, no doubt wondering why I was acting so irrationally. I wasn't handling this well, and I knew he was upset. Why couldn't I just come out and tell him and not be so secretive? I was running away from him but didn't want to. I couldn't help it; I was fleeing because that's what I'd done for so long, and it felt like the only thing I knew to do. I wanted to change but didn't know how. I wanted Dane to know but couldn't tell him.

I dove into the surf, wanting to wash away my fears.

Chapter Twenty-Five

I stood in the shower, dripping, listening to BJ hurry down the stairs, out onto the patio, and onto to the beach. What had happened? Why had she run off so fast? Had I said something wrong?

This wasn't the first time BJ had dodged personal subjects when they popped up in conversation. But this had been the first time she had physically run away. I felt I had been patient, had backed off whenever I sensed she wanted to change the subject, and had respected her privacy. Or was it secrecy? What was she being secretive about?

I toweled off, put on my trunks, and went downstairs. I stood at the window and watched her throw down her towel, take off her sunglasses and beach hat, and dash into the surf, diving into the first wave that came along.

I went into the kitchen and got a couple of cold drinks. I put them in a cooler with a couple of pieces of fruit, our typical beach diet. I went to the window and saw her head bobbing above the waves before she dove below the surface like a dolphin. I had seen her diving and swimming pattern many times, but suddenly I felt an epiphany.

BJ had been treating me the same way that she was swimming: running fast, diving in, surfacing, going down again, popping up to catch her breath, then diving out of sight. Evasive, elusive, out of reach, and moving away.

Ok, I thought. *Maybe that's a bit of a stretch.* I watched her swimming farther out to sea. I decided to leave her alone and not go out on the beach. I didn't want to engage her in conversation. Clearly, it was a dead-end discussion, and she was avoiding something about the subject.

If she needed privacy, if she had to run away, dive, and swim out of reach, I'd let her have her way.

I went over to her music cabinet and put on a couple of CDs. One of her k. d. lang's and one of my Doors. I went back to the sofa, picked up the Teddy Roosevelt biography I had been enjoying, and started to read. At first I had trouble concentrating, but I managed to get absorbed and read for a half hour before I looked up.

BJ was still swimming, doing long laps a hundred yards off shore, churning hard through the water, keeping her distance. I went back to my book and read two more chapters.

When I looked up again, BJ was dragging herself out of the surf. She had been swimming close to an hour in the ocean. She had to be exhausted. When she came out of the water, she put her hands on her hips and took deep breaths, her head lowered. After a minute or two, she resumed walking to her towel, a bit unsteady in her gait. When she got to her towel, she dropped to her knees, picked up the end, and held it to her face. She rubbed it over her wet hair, put on her floppy hat, and rolled over on her back. Her chest heaved up and down for five minutes, her legs splayed on the sand in exhaustion. If not for her chest moving up and down, she looked drowned.

What was going on in her head?

Chapter Twenty-Six

I dragged myself off the beach, lay down on my towel, and fell asleep. I had swum hard for more than an hour, trying to forget the conversation in the shower. But I kept kicking myself for being rude to Dane.

By fleeing to the beach so abruptly, I had thrown a block in front of Dane as effortlessly as a nose guard clearing a path for a halfback on a sweep play. Dane hadn't been ready and had gone down like he'd been blindsided. He was intuitive and had refrained from asking me questions when topics came up about my past. He let me avoid getting into them, and I respected him for that.

This was an important reason I felt so comfortable around him; he let me be myself and wasn't pushing or prying. I needed that in a man. He was perfect for me. But I knew I couldn't always get my way. I knew I'd have to open up sometime and share everything with him. But not yet . . . and I think he knew that. God, I hope he did. I couldn't risk losing him because of my craziness. I knew I'd have a hard time telling him how much he meant to me. Yet I needed his strength to move on and build a solid relationship.

I just couldn't tell him yet.

When I came back inside, Dane was reading on the sofa, eating a peach, and sipping iced tea.

"Hi," I said feebly, my voice a little weak from exhaustion. "Like your book?" What a lame question. I was faking it, and he knew it.

"I don't often get time to read a book for hours." I knew what that meant. He hadn't wanted to join me and was letting me work out my anxieties without distractions. Good move on his part. I wanted to be sweet to him again, but I didn't know what words to say. Plus, I was tired and needed to lie down.

"I'm beat. I swam too long. Can I get another shower and lie down for a few minutes? I promise I won't be long."

"Take as long as you want," he said. "I was going to fix up something in the kitchen. I know you're hungry."

"Am I ever. But I need to get some strength back first."

I dragged my weary self upstairs. My body ached, and I had a headache. Too much sun, too much frantic exercise, and a lousy feeling about how I had acted.

I took off my bikini, got into bed, and closed my eyes. My head was throbbing, but I knew I couldn't sleep. Dane and I needed to eat some dinner and spend some time together.

After a few minutes, I slipped out of bed and took a shower. The hot needles on my body woke me up, and I started to feel like my old self again. The hot water flowing over my body was getting out the soreness. How long had I swum? Six, eight, ten times back and forth. I must have swum close to two miles. No wonder I was beat. And hungry.

I wanted to get back downstairs and be with Dane.

I dried off and slipped on a shift, too tired to put on underwear. Dane was in the kitchen, chopping something and listening to Sinatra. He was singing along in a warbly tenor. Good for him. He wasn't going to get trapped trying to get me out of my funk. He sensed I had to do that myself.

Dane was in front of the fridge, looking at the wine selection. He took out a Sonoma Chardonnay, one of my favorites. He turned when he heard the patter of my feet on the cold tiles. I must have looked a mess.

"Hi, sleepyhead. Feeling better?" he said. "You swam a long time." He got down a couple of wineglasses and poured our wine. He had chopped tomatoes, cucumbers, celery, and Vidalia onions and put them on a tray next to cheese, olives, and meat slices.

"That looks so good," I said, taking a wineglass from him. "I'm starved."

"Want to go out on the patio? The sun's behind us now, and it's not as hot. I was going to put some pasta on the stove to heat up."

"Can we go to bed first?" I said, surprised at my directness. "I haven't been very nice to you today."

A smile came over his face.

"Don't you want to finish your wine and have a tomato?" he asked.

Chapter Twenty-Seven

Our early-evening lovemaking was slow and quiet. BJ hardly said a word, moving my hand where she wanted it, kissing my fingers, nibbling my ears, and climaxing early. She laid back and closed her eyes, and I thought I saw a tear form in one duct. She slipped out of bed and headed into her bathroom, saying, "We'd better go to dinner before I fall asleep."

We took a shower upstairs in silence, and she got out ahead of me. She was still moody after our shower, so I left her alone while I went downstairs to get dressed for dinner. The sun was going down, but it was still hot and sticky outside.

We wore high summer wear, she in a shift, no bra or make up, and stylish sandals. BJ tied a bandana in her hair so she didn't have to fool with it. I put on a Hawaiian shirt, baggy shorts, and sandals. Our tans were dark and shiny as mahogany. BJ's hair was bleached blonder than I had ever seen it, and her blue-gray eyes looked like jewels against her tan.

She had wanted to go to dinner at a French restaurant across from the courthouse square where the farmers market had been held earlier that week. She was so tired at dinner I thought she might fall asleep in her salad. We ate in silence. I knew she was struggling with more than exhaustion. I was going to let her open up at her own pace and not ask questions that might make her dive into the surf again.

I watched her toy with a piece of tomato. I could almost hear the little doors in her heart open and close, opening an inch at a time, then closing, testing to see which door would open enough that she could tell me what was going on inside.

The waiter brought our dinners, and I poured more wine.

"This is good wine. It goes well with my scampi," she said finally. A small door had opened. She forced a smile, the corners of her mouth crinkling up.

"I thought you'd like it," I responded. The door closed, and none others opened even a crack.

We picked at our food, tearing off bread, sipping wine, moving food around on our plates. It was the longest we had been together without conversation. Our talks had been relaxed and open-ended, starting off on one topic and veering off in all directions, both of us marveling at how easy it was to shift and move into areas with ease. It had been that way from the start; we were relaxed and comfortable listening to each other, never rushing the other one, never bored, and genuinely interested in what was coming out of our mouths.

I knew that relationships didn't always flow in a linear course; they spin off in one direction or another, come to dead ends, start over, and find the thread again. The important thing was to keep the flow going and let it find its own course. Time and patience would get our thoughts and emotions on the same plane.

Suddenly she asked me a question about something she hadn't expressed interest in before.

"When will you go back to work?"

"Monday." She nodded and nibbled on the tomato.

"It's been a good week for us," she said. A more promising door was opening. "I've enjoyed being with you every minute. You make it seem so easy." She looked up and smiled, her eyes twinkling in the candlelight. She looked tired, and her cheeks seemed to droop.

BJ put down her fork and put her hands in her lap. "We should say goodbye tomorrow afternoon. I have a very busy week ahead of me. Tomorrow night, Barbara and I are getting together. We haven't had a day together in . . . oh, a long, long time. We have so much to catch up on. Tomorrow's the only time we have to get together; she leaves Monday."

I nodded. "I understand. I should head back tomorrow afternoon as well. It's a half-day drive to St. Francis." Then she said something that surprised me.

"My dad and his family are arriving Monday for a week at the beach."

"Oh, I didn't know that." A door that I didn't even know about had opened wide.

"I know. I haven't talked much about him. My father and I . . . have had some difficult times since Mom died."

Again, an important fact she had hidden from me before. She had occasionally mentioned her mother but not that she was dead.

"After Mom died, Dad went back to France, where he's from, and married a French woman with younger children. His wife has been cool toward me and hasn't completely accepted me or Dad's life in America. They occasionally come and spend a week here. It's a little stressful when she's here; I try to make the best of it. A cleaning crew is coming tomorrow afternoon to get ready for them. Dad's new wife always wants the house spotless."

She had mentioned that her Dad was French and lived in Paris with his second wife, but these additional details were new to me. I realized now why she had become moody and quiet today. She had the next week on her mind, along with saying goodbye to me. We had talked about many things, but not the details of her father's life and its effect on her. Pain and loss seemed to be her constant companions.

BJ looked down at her plate and continued to move her food around. She nibbled on the end of her bread, taking birdlike pecks, avoiding my eyes.

"When will we see each other again?" she asked, still not looking up from her plate.

"Soon, I hope. When would you like?" I said.

She pursed her lips together, keeping her eyes away from mine. "How about next July again?" she said, finally looking up at me, her eyes moist.

Not what I wanted to hear. "Why so long?" I asked. "I live only a few hours away. Aren't you coming back before then?"

She shook her head. "I don't think I will."

"You'll stay in Seattle all year?"

She nodded. "Most of the time. I think it's for the best. I want to do a good job. It means a lot to be back teaching kids again. It was a very important part of my life before, and I want it back. Very much."

I swallowed hard. "Can I come see you?"

It looked like her face was going to crack. Her eyes were blinking, tears about to flow, and she put her hand on mine.

"I want to be with you more, Dane, but not until next year. I know it sounds like a long time, but if we wait, we can plan to be together more. A lot more. I need to go back to teaching again without distractions. I'm juggling two important issues: having you in my life, and starting back to work. It's unfortunate that we're separated by a whole country, but we can't do anything about that for now. I feel so lucky to have found you. You're the one who got me started on my life again. I have to show myself I can be on my own so I can be with you for the rest of my life. I couldn't go back to work unless I knew there was a reason to have a full life again. And that life is with you. Forever. Oh, I know this sounds strange, but please try to understand."

It did sound strange. Mixed up. But if I tried to pry, she could fall apart in the restaurant, with the candles burning and the waiters scurrying about looking busy and very continental.

I knew how hard it had been for BJ to tell me about the struggles she'd been going through. We had become so much closer this summer, and next summer we could actually start talking about sharing our lives together. But waiting a full year wasn't what I wanted. Last summer had been so carefree and fun, getting to know each other and becoming lovers. This summer our week had shown us that it was not a brief summer affair, but a relationship that had a future. If we could wait another year, we would never have to be apart again.

I looked at her, knowing it would be a full year until I could look into those eyes again. Until I could share my feelings and not fear she would dive deep and never resurface.

"You won't forget me in another year's time?" I asked.

A sad smile appeared on her beautiful face. "You remember the double shooting star we saw?"

I struggled to smile back at her. "Of course I do."

"I could never forget you, Dane, any more than I could forget that incredible double meteor we saw together."

I took a deep breath and said, "Ok. Next July. July 20. Same beach house. Better movies and new music. Farmers market and who knows what else. I hope it's longer than a week."

"It will be," she reassured me. "That's what I want. And the time will be right then. I want to talk about spending our lives together."

"I hope the time flies," I said, knowing how brave it sounded but recognizing what agony I would have to live through for the next twelve months.

With tears in her eyes, she reached over to touch my lips. "So do I, Dane. I'll be ready next summer."

Chapter Twenty-Eight

It was harder than I imagined it would be. I had been brave and valiant, telling her I would agree to her terms and not see her or talk with her for a full year until we could be together, never leaving each other again.

I felt depressed and lonely like I never had in my life. I showed up at work the next week and listened to everyone rave about my beautiful tan and relaxed appearance. I put on a brave face and hinted about beach parties, beautiful bikini-clad women, steamy passion, martinis at the country club, golf, tennis, and romantic moonlight walks until I was sick of it myself.

By October, my tan had faded. I lost weight even though I hadn't shown up at the gym since July. I tried to focus on work, but my mind was a few hundred miles south, where the weather was hot and humid, waves crashed ashore, and summer never ended.

Leaves turned red and gold, but I barely noticed. Baseball season gave way to football, and I didn't catch a single game.

Basketball came, and I went to a few games but couldn't remember who had won by the time I walked out of the arena.

I went home to visit my parents for Christmas. My mother kept mentioning that I shouldn't be alone for the holidays, asking if I hadn't found a nice young woman in Shattuck yet with a good job and a nice family. I left before New Year's, faking job responsibility, and spent New Year's Eve by myself, drinking champagne, looking at the clock and then the calendar, and wondering why time passed so slowly.

I reflected on the previous New Year's, when Jenna had thrown down the gauntlet, demanding a marriage proposal. I had looked at her and tried to imagine how I would tell her I was never going to ask her to marry me. In the end, she had stormed out of the room in anger, yanking off the pearl necklace I had given her and tossing it behind her. It had slid across the carpet of the condo. It had settled on the socks I had taken off the previous night while we had sat on the sofa and she had kept mentioning how disappointing the holiday had been and I had kept looking at the clock on the wall.

I imagine some people would say I was a coward for not having told her the reason. I rationalized that it was better for her emotional well-being to be the one who stormed out, so she could tell her friends and family she had broken off the relationship. One day Jenna would find a nice man to settle down with, raise a family, and be happy. At least having a former fiancé break up with her because he had fallen in love with another woman would be a pain she would never have to live with.

I was relieved when I received a note from Gus on my birthday. He wished me the best, said he'd had a good report from his last prostate exam, and reminded me that he'd help out if I was interested in a real estate investment with him. He'd have a couple hundred thousand free by the end of the year and would look at any deals I might be considering. Not a word about Jenna.

Winter was long and lonely. The only pleasure was tearing off the monthly page from the calendar on my bedroom dresser. I went skiing in February with a group from the office. We stayed at a lodge with a gang of singles, marrieds, older, younger, pretty, ugly, and several shades. I was comfortable in a group setting; I could mingle among them and not spend much time with any one person or tribe. That was my goal: blend and disappear.

It didn't work. Single girls hit on me, married women hit on me, and guys hit on me. I was surprised by the universal assault on my body. Here I was, single, trying to be fun-loving, an average skier, not a bad storyteller, reasonably good-looking, no bad breath, not balding, with an easygoing temperament. But that week I seemed to be the trophy they all wanted mounted on the mantle over the fireplace that they could brag they'd bagged.

I managed to slip away from all of them. I was having none of their ski trip conjugal conquests. I'd put up with their initial attempts, once they had me in their sights, but I determined to escape their snares and avoid listening to their lonely stories. I also avoided fitting into plans for further games once we returned to work. My world and theirs simply would never meet. I had had enough of those games in high school and college.

By March, I couldn't handle the loneliness. I drove down to BJ's house one cold and rainy weekend, listening to jazz on the radio, watching wind and rain fly across the road and over my windshield, faking the flu at the office so I could escape and get a little relief from my loneliness by returning to BJ's beach house, if only for a few hours.

I was proud of myself for upholding BJ's wishes. No phone calls. No letters. No contact until July. Yes, she felt there was a good reason she needed the distance, and I had to honor that. I wondered if BJ knew how hard this was on me. But it didn't matter; this was the mountain I had to climb, and I would do it to reach the summit in July.

The road to her house was muddy and filled with pot-holes. I drove slowly, driving up on the grassy patches when I encountered a large puddle in the road. In the summer, this was a patch of sand hard as cement. In the winter, it was oatmeal.

Rain had coated the beach house. The gray wood was almost black, with water streaming down from the roof and splashing onto the sandy soil. I stepped around the puddles and made it to the overhang above the back door.

I reached into my pocket and took out my most cherished possession. The purloined key. I had not told BJ about it the previous summer. I could talk to a therapist for years and probably get hours of analysis about why I had hidden this significant detail from her. But I didn't care what he or anyone else said about the purloined key. It was my one connection to BJ when we were apart, and I wasn't going to give it up. It was my only connection to our past and future.

As soon as I walked into the garage, I felt sad. The boating and fishing equipment looked abandoned. The air inside was cold and damp. For the first time, I felt like an intruder. The house had been a sanctuary for me during the two past summers. Now it was like a temple that I had invaded.

I felt uncomfortable but moved toward the main part of the house. The rain and clouds made it seem dark as a dungeon. Instead of being comforted, I felt ill at ease. Why was I there? It was not my home; I had been an infrequent guest. Yes, BJ and I had slept together there, made love, and talked for hours. But she was not there, and I knew shouldn't be either.

Sheets covered the sofas and chairs; drapes covered the sliding glass door. I couldn't get the warm, familiar feeling I'd had there with BJ. Her father's family had been here the week after I had left, and a different mood had settled over the house. It was still there.

I looked up at the second floor. Instead of being light and airy from all the windows, it was in shadows. The doors to the bedrooms were shut. Instead of inviting me, they were excluding me.

The air was chilly and lifeless. A tremor ran through my body. I had to leave. I turned around and headed outside. I could not be there without BJ by my side.

Chapter Twenty-Nine

I felt queasy during a Valentine's Day school party. The children had decorated cards, cut out designs, pasted them onto posters, and made individual Valentines. The kids also helped me bake cookies to hand out at the party for parents the next day.

In the school kitchen while we were the baking cookies that afternoon, I felt woozy and again thought I was going to throw up. I went to the bathroom and sat in a stall with my head between my knees. I felt faint and nauseous. I rationalized it was the tacos I had had for lunch. I left school, went home to bed, and slept through the night.

The next day I felt fine. No sign of nausea. A twenty-four-hour bug. The Valentine's party was lively fun, and many parents came up and thanked Nancy and me for making it a special time. I ate two cupcakes, went home, and vomited them up at midnight.

I quit going to the gym that week and hurried home every afternoon from class, exhausted, with weird thoughts going through my mind. I'd sleep from six in the evening until six the next morning, usually waking up fresh and ready to start the day. Most days were good. Others not so.

Sometime in March, I fainted in class as I was beginning a reading exercise. Nancy rushed to my side, and I remember seeing her face looking down at me, her lips moving, but I couldn't hear a word. I lost consciousness and didn't regain it until the ambulance was speeding down the highway. I looked up at the young man dressed in medical garb and babbled: "When the sun came over the horizon, the geese flew and began their flight to Canada, where they would spend the summer and lay eggs . . ." I didn't know where those words came from. I didn't even remember saying them but was told about it later in the day in the hospital, where I lay with an IV sticking out of my arm.

The principal, Mr. Wiggins, had gone with me in the ambulance, holding my hand and looking down at me, stroking my head and saying, "That's a good story, BJ. The kids will like it when you tell them." His eyes flicked between mine and the medical person who was shining a light in my eyes and checking my pulse and blood pressure.

I didn't go back to school but remained in the hospital. Nurses and doctors came every day, looking with lights into my eyes, checking my hearing, and sending me off to take tests in cold rooms with gray equipment that whirred and made clanking noises as they took pictures of my brain. I felt like a cell being examined by giant microscopes that could see things in my body I couldn't. What did they see? When would they tell me?

The headaches came. Powerful, heavy pressure, like vises squeezing my brain. The pain would become so intense I would pass out. Light was a trigger for the pain. If a sliver of light got past the shade on my window, I could feel the pressure build and pound on my brain until the nurse came in and slipped me more pain medication through my IV.

Some mornings, I'd wake up and not want to face the pain that would come that day. The really horrible pain didn't happen every day, but often enough to make me tremble and sweat as soon as my eyes opened.

My brother and his wife came; it seemed like they were by my side for several days. Various people came into my room and talked about me when my eyes were closed. I could hear them and didn't like what they were saying. My eyes were closed because of the light, but my ears worked fine. They used the terms *caretaker, custodial care, surgery, drugs, experimental tests, extreme measures.* I was afraid and prayed every time I woke up. I prayed to go back to my life in the classroom and get ready to go to the beach. It was only a few months away. Dane would be there! He would talk to me, make me laugh, and love me. I wanted that very much. It was what I was living for. I finally had a reason to live again.

They fed me through a tube when I was unconscious for long periods of time. They washed my body daily. A pretty young nurse came in to check my charts and monitors, and she would chat endlessly about her cats. I slept more than I was awake, and I lost track of time. My memory was vague and fleeting. When the pain came, it was relentless, except when pain medication went through my IV and dripped into my veins.

A severe headache woke me in the middle of the night. Hammers were pounding in my head for hours and hours. More fluid slipped into my veins, and I slept again.

One day they lifted me off my bed and put me on a gurney. They wheeled me down a marble corridor, and I could hear beeping of monitors and smell pungent chemical odors. I woke up some time later, bundled in warm covers. They wheeled me into an ambulance and drove off. It was very dark. Something was wrapped over my head and eyes. I heard a loud engine and felt myself lifted into an airplane. *Where are they taking me? Who told them to send me? Why are they taking me someplace?* I was terrified but couldn't cry out. Fluid kept dripping into my arm. I felt motion all around me but didn't know what it was.

When I opened my eyes, Simms and Mattie were standing beside my bed. Mattie squeezed my hand; Simms ran his sweaty palm over my forehead, saying, "There, there, BJ. We're here to look after you now. You're home where you belong. People who love you will look after you now."

I went to sleep, comforted that I was near my beach house. Was Dane there? Would he come? When would I see him again?

Chapter Thirty

The last two weeks had been stressful. I had worked hard all spring, completing an important assignment and getting all sorts of accolades from my bosses and peers. My performance had slumped when I'd returned from the beach the previous July. After going through my winter funk, I had seen the proverbial light at the end of the tunnel and wanted to go into the summer with work behind me and a two-week vacation for visiting BJ. I had put in plenty of overtime, and no one was going to object to my asking for the time off.

My boss came into my office the Friday before I left. He pumped my hand and thanked me for all of my work on his pet project.

"I know you've got a special place at the beach. And there's a rumor there's a lovely lady you might be seeing." He winked, not in a salacious way, but just to let me know he wished me well in my personal life. "Have fun, get plenty of sun, and come back for a rousing third quarter. We've got great plans for you in our operations, Dane. I think you'll be happy when we make some changes in September."

I thanked him, cleared off my desk, and took business cards of special clients to call on the road with updates. I had packed my bags the night before but didn't want to leave until the morning. Traffic would be murder if I left at six on a Friday evening, and I'd be exhausted by the time I arrived. If I left at six the next morning, I'd get to BJ's around eleven, fresh and ready to have the best summer vacation of my life. She and I had agreed on July 20, and that was Saturday. I wanted to prove to myself and to BJ that I'd deliver exactly what I'd promised.

I rolled out of my condo at five forty-five the next morning, a cup of steaming coffee in the cup holder and a bagel and cream cheese on the seat next to me. I tuned in my classic rock station, tapping the wheel to a favorite Clapton riff, and hit the turnpike right at six. I was in heaven!

I stopped for breakfast and a bathroom break around eight, and made another stop around ten, only an hour from BJ's. I went into the bathroom, changed into shorts and a Hawaiian shirt, filled the car with gas, and drove off for the last lonely hour of my summer. The traffic on the interstate was light, and I resisted pressing the pedal and risking a speeding ticket. No worries; I'd have the rest of the summer ahead of me. Might as well relax and enjoy the beautiful weather.

All morning I had been contemplating how the vacation would be with BJ. I was convinced we would pick up where we'd left off last year and have two unforgettable weeks together. I'd invite her to come up to Shattuck in August. I assumed she would be going back to Seattle to teach at the end of August, so I wanted her to see my world. I looked forward to talking about how and when we could get together over the next year. I wanted to visit her in the fall and then spend the holidays together, possibly in Mexico or Hawaii. I certainly wanted this to be the summer we started to bring our lives and careers together, as BJ had indicated we would do. Going a year without seeing each other was a killer. Never again. I'd do anything to be closer to her—even move to Seattle if I couldn't have her come and live with me. There were lots of important life issues to discuss, and I couldn't wait. It's what had kept me going during those long, cold, dark winter nights alone.

I pulled off the highway at the unmarked road and made my way down the asphalt to the point where it turned into sand. I could see BJ's house over the dunes between the trees. I was so excited! My heart was pounding and my hands sweating. In just minutes, I'd have her in my arms again. I'd be kissing her beautiful face and feeling her breath on my cheek. *Heaven.* I sang off-key to an old Willie Nelson road song. Life was great again: BJ was waiting. Summer was finally here!

When I pulled into the clearing, I was surprised to see two cars parked behind the house. A black Mercedes and a tan Audi. But not BJ's car. The curtains in the study were open. I half-expected to see BJ peek out and run down to meet me. But her beautiful face did not appear.

I got out of the car and walked to the back door. My purloined key was in my pocket, but I wasn't going to use it. I smiled to myself; this would be the time I would tell her my little secret. We'd have a good laugh, reminiscing about our first summer together, my ankle sprain, her dropping the keys, my finding one, putting it my pocket, and forgetting to tell her about it.

The back door was unlocked. I opened it and saw that the beach gear was in the same place it had been when I'd come for my brief visit in March. Nothing had been moved. Again, I expected BJ to appear at the door and great me warmly.

I heard voices inside. *Was someone else visiting BJ?*

I opened the door. Still no BJ. Three people were seated on the sofa. They rose and came over to meet me. I recognized two of them.

Simms and Mattie Russell. The third person was a dark-skinned man in his thirties who looked slightly Asian.

What are they doing here? And where is BJ?

Simms moved toward me. He wore a dark suit, white shirt, and navy tie. His face was somber. Mattie, wearing a black dress, came behind Simms and stood to his side as he shook my hand. "Hello, Dane. Simms Russell. We met last summer." His eyes revealed sadness.

The Asian man stood back at the sofa, his hands folded in front of him.

What was going on? Where was BJ? What were these people doing in her house?

"Of course, Simms. I remember. We came to your party. Hello, Mattie. Where's BJ?"

Mattie came closer. Her eyes were red. I sensed she wanted to embrace me but was holding back.

Simms's voice was low and cracking. "Son, would you come in and have a seat? We have to have a talk."

"Where's BJ? She's supposed to be here. . . . Has something happened?" I was blubbering, my voice breaking. *Where is BJ?*

My pulse was racing, my mind reeling. Something was wrong. I felt I might faint from the shock of not seeing BJ and finding these people in her home. *Why are Simms and Mattie here? And who is the other man?*

I moved warily to the center of the house and sat in a chair next to the sofa, where Mattie and Simms had returned.

They were sitting on the sofa where BJ and I had made love, eaten dinners, and talked for hours into the night, naked in the dark. It was *our* sofa; I couldn't believe they were there and BJ wasn't.

"Son . . . this is a very hard time for all of us," Simms started. I shrank down into the chair, not liking what he was saying.

"Dane . . . I'm sorry to say that BJ died last month." Tears were in his eyes. Mattie reached for his arm, tears running down her cheeks.

I bolted out of the chair and stood up. I couldn't sit still. What was he saying? I couldn't believe his words . . . they were so awful!

"What!" I yelled. "What do you mean?" I was screaming. "No, no, don't say that. Where is she? I want to see her. Now! I know she's in the house! Where is she?"

My body began trembling, my hands waving, my arms shaking. My legs felt weak, but I moved around in jerky motions, back and forth. I felt I was going to explode.

Mattie rose and moved toward me, reaching to take me in her arms. She held me, and I could feel myself shaking in her embrace.

She sobbed, "Dane, Dane, I'm so sorry. Please sit down. We loved BJ like our own daughter. This is so sad, I can't believe it. But she's not with us anymore."

We stood in the middle of the living room, me shaking, Mattie holding me. Our bodies quivered, and she held me tighter. It was such an odd and terrifying experience. One minute I'm expecting to hold my lover, and next minute I'm being consoled by an older woman I barely know.

Mattie reached down for my hand. "Here, Dane, let's sit on the sofa. Let Simms tell you. We've been waiting all morning for you to come. Please sit here between me and Simms."

She guided me to the sofa like I was a small child. I followed her and sat where she placed me. She held my hand in both of hers and squeezed tightly.

Simms cleared his throat. "Dane, this is the hardest thing I've ever had to do in my life. Mattie and I were very close to BJ. She was like a daughter. She and Barbara were like sisters. We have been grieving like parents since BJ passed away."

I couldn't grasp what Simms was saying. BJ was supposed to be here, now, waiting for me like we scheduled a year ago. My mind was racing with the horrible consequences of what Simms was saying.

"I don't believe it. I don't believe it," I repeated over and over, my voice cracking and tears flowing. Mattie held my hand, the only comfort I felt. "What . . . what happened . . . what happened to her?"

Simms cleared his throat and started again, looking into my eyes.

"BJ had a brain tumor. She suffered headaches and dizzy spells this spring when she was teaching. One day she fainted and was taken to a hospital. They ran tests that showed she had a brain tumor. Deep in her brain."

Mattie held my hand tightly as he continued.

"In April, we got a call from a doctor in Seattle who said BJ had a health care directive that said we should be contacted in case of emergency. I had actually written the directive for her last summer when we updated her will and trust. I was surprised that she wanted us to be contacted instead of her family in Arizona, but she explained at the time that she wouldn't want to burden her brother and his wife, as they had three small children and were on overload."

"But . . . but . . . why didn't anyone contact me?" I stammered.

"We thought of it, Dane, but we were so busy getting ready to have BJ come back. All we thought about was getting her comfortable in the hospital. And once she arrived, it was nip and tuck, day after day of waiting by her bedside. She was in and out of comas, conscious and unconscious, coherent and incoherent. We were trying to adjust to her deteriorating condition. Our first and only priority was taking care of BJ. Your name came up, but when we talked to BJ about you, she'd have a spell and we had to just be there with her. I . . . I know this is hard to understand. But those days were very hard on Mattie and me. And Barbara. She was here the last week."

"And what happened?" I managed to ask again.

Simms looked down at his shoes, over at Mattie, and then at me. "The brain tumor . . . they found out . . . was inoperable. They did exploratory surgery and found it was too large and had spread into areas in the brain that would be destroyed if they tried to take out." He shook his head and looked away.

Mattie spoke. "Dane, know you meant a lot to BJ. How long had you known her?"

"We met two years ago. We spent a few days here at the beach house, and I came back again last summer. That's when I met you and we went to your party."

She nodded and looked over at Simms. "Did you know about her . . . past? Her family?"

"You mean her husband and daughter dying in the accident?"

Mattie nodded. "Yes. A terrible, terrible event. Tragic. I don't see how anyone could come back after losing their spouse and young child. I certainly couldn't have."

"What Mattie's trying to say, Dane, is that the tragedy of losing her family sent BJ on a terrible spiral downward. It wasn't just her immediate family. She had also lost her mother. Losing her family was a terrible shock for her. She had a history of depression when she was younger, and she'd received psychiatric treatment. After she had Sylvia, she experienced postpartum depression and spent a few days in the hospital. When Brad and Sylvia died, she couldn't go back to work and had a very hard time. And then the miscarriage. Losing her unborn baby boy sent her into another deep depression. She was hospitalized, had a year of psychiatric treatment, and was on antidepressants. She was coming out of it when her mother died of a heart attack. Again, she ended up in the hospital for another six months."

Simms picked up where Mattie left off. "She was getting back to her old self when she met you. She was so happy to have found a man who knew nothing about her past and could love her for who she was. She wanted to protect you from knowing about her severe bouts with depression and hospitalization because she feared it might scare you away. That's what she was afraid of. So if there were gaps that you might have noticed, that is what they were. She felt she was protecting you by not confiding about her dark shadows.

"We saw her after you left, when her father and his family came for a week. Her father, Maurice, and I had been business partners. But more importantly, our families were close. Mattie and Elaine were best friends. Their family's tragedies hit our family very hard."

I still couldn't believe what I was hearing. I had so many questions but had to hear everything that Simms said. His eyes were moist, and small beads of sweat were on his forehead. He wrung his hands and wiped them on his pants. I smelled a hint of his pleasant leathery aftershave.

"When we were contacted by the Seattle surgeon, we hired a private jet to fly BJ to our university hospital. It's very good and has excellent surgeons. They did more tests and confirmed that her tumor was inoperable and growing. She had a few months left, at best. She was heavily medicated against the headaches and was not conscious for long stretches. Mattie and I alternated at the hospital, waiting for her to come out of the coma. When she did, she'd give us directions on what she wanted. She arranged her funeral. She told us who to contact and what to say. She asked me to make alterations to her will and trust, and she signed those days before she died."

Mattie loosened her grip on my hand and put one hand on my shoulder. "Simms, is this the right time to talk about this? You've told him the most terrible news he's ever heard. It's too early to start talking about the legal stuff. There's plenty of time later. Can't we wait? Let's let Dane talk."

"Dane, darling," she said, her face so close to mine that I could smell her lilac and powder. "Please, do you have questions? We're here to help you."

I was in shock and denial. I half-expected and deeply wished to look up and see BJ bounding down the stairs in her bikini and sun hat, running out to the patio and onto the beach. I could picture her so clearly, even now, while listening to Simms and Mattie tell me I would never see her again.

"I . . . I don't know what to say . . . no, wait. . . . Tell me, did she suffer?"

Simms's brow furrowed. "Son, she had excellent doctors, and they treated her well. They prescribed painkillers when her headaches were unbearable. When we talked, she did not seem in pain. She was lucid for long periods, so we could discuss whatever she wanted. She gave us very explicit instructions on all sorts of personal, family, and financial details. Her brother came and was by her side for a week. Her father came from France. Barbara came at the end; they talked for hours. So she was able to talk with everyone she wanted."

"Did she mention me?"

"Of course she did, son. But she didn't want you here. We talked about you many times, but she was emphatic that she didn't want you to see her in that condition. We wanted to contact you and have you come. She refused, and we had to honor her request. She told us your plans to come today, and she wanted you to find out from us after she was gone, and not see her with her head shaved, weak, thin, and . . . and dying."

Simms cleared his throat. She did say one thing that puzzled me, but she said you would understand. She said, "Remember the meteor."

It was all I could do at that point not to start crying. Instead, I changed the subject.

"Who is that man?" I asked, glancing at the distinguished-looking gentleman who had been quiet all along. Simms turned to him.

"Dane, this is Gerald Elea. He was BJ's financial advisor in town. She wanted him to be here when we saw you."

"Why?"

"Simms," Mattie protested. "Should we . . . ?"

"Yes, it's all right now, dear." Simms turned to face me. BJ made alterations to her trust. She gifted the beach house to you. She said it would mean more to you than to anyone in her family. Her father had given it to her when he moved to France, and she wanted you to inherit it."

I was too stunned to speak.

"She also left assets to you that Gerald will tell you about."

Mr. Elea cleared his throat. "Mr. Chambers, I managed BJ's retirement accounts. She asked me to draw up papers to transfer them to you upon her death."

"Dane, did you know BJ's family was wealthy?" Simms asked.

"Well, I guess I knew they were somewhat prosperous. BJ and I didn't really talk about things like that. I thought the beach house belonged to the family."

"Her father gifted it to her two years ago," Simms said. "There were . . . other family issues with his French wife, issues that were resolved in BJ's favor. She wanted you to inherit the house and have enough assets to keep it up. Mr. Elea will tell you about that."

"Yes, you inherited her retirement accounts, which total about a hundred thousand dollars. When you come to my office, we can have them transferred to your accounts."

I didn't know how many shocks I could handle in one day.

"I don't care about BJ's money. I just want her back!" I was in tears.

Later that afternoon, Simms, Mattie, and I went out to the beach, where the sun was behind us now. Clouds were building up over the horizon, possibly bringing a warm summer rain tomorrow. It was hot and sticky, like other July afternoons I had spent there. I wore my sandals; Simms and Mattie had taken off their dress shoes and walked barefoot across the warm sand. Mattie had her arm linked in mine. I put my hand over hers, and we walked somewhat unsteadily toward the surf.

Simms carried in both hands a pewter urn the size of a flower vase. He said BJ had asked for me to be at the ceremony where her ashes would be sprinkled in the ocean. We stopped in dry sand a few feet from the highest point the waves had spilled on shore. We watched in silence as several waves came ashore, rushing toward us, spilling lacy foam over the beach. It was a beautiful afternoon, and I could almost picture BJ out in the waves, her arms chopping through the water, looking up to wave at me and motion me to come in after her.

Simms cleared his throat.

"Dear, do you want to see if Dane would like to say something?"

"Yes."

I was still in shock from all I had heard that afternoon. I couldn't imagine a word to say. They waited patiently. Simms held the urn in both hands. Mattie clung to my side.

I wasn't good at public praying and didn't know if this was the time to pray or offer an intimate comment.

"Goodbye forever, BJ. Until I join you here."

Chapter Thirty-One

I opened the garage door the following July with strong, mixed feelings. My overwhelming feeling was fear that I would have such a powerful reaction that I could not stay in BJ's house without having a breakdown.

I parked where BJ had always parked, behind the door by the northwest corner. I used my purloined key and went in through the back door. The sailboat, kayaks, surfboards, fishing boats, tackle, and diving gear were all in their places. The parking spot in the garage was empty. I entered the house and stood in the kitchen. It was dim but not morbid. And silent. I could hear a slight breeze coming from the ocean.

The kitchen was spotless. The dining and living rooms had not changed since the previous year when Simms, Mattie, and the financial guy had told me the horrible news. The heavy drapes over the sliding glass door to the patio had been replaced with lighter ones that allowed light from the beach to filter through. I could see the surf through the gauzy drape. I had my first pleasant thought; I would go onto the beach that morning.

The refrigerator was completely cleaned out; not even a juice container. I'd have go to the grocery store to get things for my week. The cabinets were clean and full of BJ's dining china, cups, and wineglasses. The silverware was all in place in the drawers. I checked below one cabinet and found large pottery and serving platters for Thanksgiving, Christmas, and special occasions.

I went out on the patio for my first clear view of the beach. The breeze was brisk, warm, and tangy. I breathed deeply and remembered the first time I had walked out on that patio with BJ, one morning three years ago. Had it been that long ago? Had it been so recent?

I walked up the stairs to the second-story bedrooms and study. The carpets had been shampooed. No sign of the red wine spill BJ had made the last time we were there.

I almost wished it were there, as a reminder of another memory.

My heart was pounding, and I had a sense of dread going into her bedroom. The bed was covered with a different bedspread. Brown with geometric designs. Strange. Who had put that there? I pulled it back and saw yellow and blue sheets, not BJ's favorite beige ones. I'd find them and put them back on. I wanted to sleep on her sheets again, even if she were not with me.

Her pictures were all in place. I looked at them, top to bottom, left to right. BJ's grandparents' and parents' wedding pictures and early family pictures. Second row, BJ and her brother growing up, graduation, wedding pictures. Third row was BJ with Brad and Sylvia. Fourth row, her adult years with her parents and beach photos on her mother's birthday. My heart was still pounding hard, and I had tears in my eyes as I scanned the photos, always coming back to those of BJ in Seattle with Brad and Sylvia. But my favorite was the one of the two of us standing by the sailboat on our trip to Gull Point. I took it down and walked over to her dresser. I leaned it against the wall and decided that would be its new permanent place.

I unlocked the sliding glass door and went out to the deck where we'd had our candlelight dinner after our sailing trip and other times as well. I ran my hand over the rail where BJ had lined up the candles so we could eat at out there at dusk, smelling of salt, the ocean, sweat, sunblock, and desire.

I had quit my job in the spring. I'd sold my condo, said goodbye to my boss and colleagues, and left with vague comments about moving to the beach and starting a new life. I had gone home and told my parents more about BJ and about my move to the beach.

In the brief times I'd spent in Cabot's Harbor, I'd met a few people and would engage with them once again. Simms and Mattie could help make some more introductions. They had been so patient and compassionate with me the previous summer and had invited me to stay with them for a few days. I had accepted, as I'd had a two-week vacation and no place else to go. I hadn't wanted to return to St. Francis after hearing of BJ's death, and I just couldn't stay at the beach house right away. They had told me stories about BJ, her family, and their history. I had become so close to Simms and Mattie that I almost felt like a member of their family. Simms had invited me to his country club and introduced me to his friends. We'd gone to lunch in town, and everyplace we went, he was greeted warmly. I had met lawyers, doctors, professors, pastors, politicians, merchants, farmers, and people from all walks of life. Simms had told me the history of his hometown and how so many generations seemed to return to this special place where they had grown up.

The last night I'd stayed with Simms and Mattie, we had eaten dinner on the patio of their lovely home. As the last foursome walked the eighteenth fairway to the clubhouse, we had looked out over the ocean at dusk. Simms had said to me, "Dane, although the circumstances were very unfortunate, we certainly have enjoyed having you stay with us these past few days. You're a fine man, and we know how much you meant to BJ. We'd like you to think about returning someday and making Cabot's Harbor your home. You own BJ's beach house now, and it would be a nice place to start a new life. We'd help you any way we could."

I had been speechless. Overcome with grief and sharing stories about BJ, I hadn't thought of my future other than returning to Shattuck and going back to work. That had been so unpleasant that I'd avoided thinking about it.

Mattie had said, "Simms and I have talked about this, Dane, and we hope you'll take us seriously. I have to admit, we are being a little selfish. As you know, our children have all grown up, married, and moved away. We see them as much as we can, but it's not the same as having them here in Cabot's Harbor. If you were here, you'd be like family to us. We enjoy your company and welcome you into our home anytime."

They both had smiled, and I could tell they were sincere. "Don't worry, son," Simms added. "We wouldn't be looking over your shoulder or prying into your life in any way. But it would be nice for Mattie and me to know that you're living in BJ's home, like she wanted. It's the closest we could get to still having her here. Think about it. We'd love to have you consider it."

And I had. All winter. I had decided at New Year's and had come down to tell them in person. I'd said that I would start making the adjustment by taking a few courses at the college during the summer—music, French, or maybe drama. I'd look for a job in the fall, and Simms had said he'd help by making introductions.

"We have some fine companies, and more are moving here every year," he had said. "I know you'll find one to your liking."

Of course, moving to Cabot's Harbor also meant living in BJ's house. It came with pleasant memories and deep sadness that she wasn't there. My strong mixed feelings about living in the beach house had been behind my taking so long to decide to move. BJ had made this new life possible, but it certainly came with emotional consequences.

I finally had resolved the dilemma by going back to what BJ did. She'd given me a gift. When a loved one gives you a gift, you ought to cherish it and bring it into your life. I had decided to honor BJ's gift by living in her beach house, starting a new life in the town she had loved, and meeting the people she had known.

One sad lesson I had learned from BJ was that life is brief. We must reach for happiness at every chance that comes to us. BJ had, and look at what we'd had together, as brief as our time had been. It did bring me happiness to know that I would be living where she had lived, sharing her home, friends, and love of the beach. I expected that, over time, I would embrace many of her values at a even deeper level: trust, daily joys, intimacy, and gracious acceptance of what life offers.

I went back inside to face a task that I had thought about every day. I went to the hutch and opened the drawer where BJ had kept her keys. Inside were two of the replacement keys she had bought the afternoon of my bike spill. I reached into my pocket and took out the keys Simms had given me that morning: the cleaning crew's and BJ's. Simms had kept one key, at my insistence. My key chain held the sixth key.

I lined up the keys on the dresser. BJ's key was the only brass one; all the spares were silver. My purloined key would remain on my key chain. The two spares would go back to their place. I put Simms's and the cleaning crew's keys in the top drawer. I took a small jewelry box from BJ's bedroom that she had used for earrings and rings. The inside was covered in blue satin. I placed BJ's key on the satin, closed the box, and put it back.

It's a funny thing about everyday objects like keys. They serve a purpose, opening and locking doors to cars and homes. We pay scant attention to them, using them, losing them, replacing them. They are ordinary objects with little emotion attachment.

It will never be that way with BJ's keys. I will use my purloined one; the others will be in the drawer until I give them out.

I expect one day I will meet a woman, bring her here, and tell her BJ's story. She will join my life. She will get one of the keys. If we have children, when they are the right age, I will give them one each. That might be two or three; I don't know. Each time I give them a key, I will tell them the story of the keys.

One key will never leave its place. BJ's will stay in her jewelry box with the blue satin. I will take it out occasionally, roll it around in my fingers, kiss it, and remember the day I spilled tea on BJ's arm and she invited me to her beach house to swim. It had been a hot July day, one of the most precious of my life. Her spontaneous invitation had changed my life forever, just as she had said it had changed her own life.

BJ is not with me in person, but she is in spirit. Each time I enter her house, see the familiar setting, walk up the stairs, go into her bedroom, or walk out on the patio, I will feel her spirit with me. I will hear her soothing voice and throaty laugh, feel her gentle touch and warm embrace. *She is a part of me.* I will share her house for the rest of my life. I know that sometimes I will carry on an internal conversation with her, remarking about the weather, how my day is going, how much I miss her, how certain things remind me of her, and how I wish she were with me.

Most of all, I will gaze up at the night sky and wonder if I will ever see another double meteor like that one.

Like now. BJ, let's get on our swimsuits and go to the beach. It will be our first swim of the summer.

THE END

Thank you for reading *A Streak Across the Sky*. I hope you'll consider writing a review and posting on this site.

My latest book is *No One Sleeps*, the sequel to *Thirteen Days in Milan* featuring the anti-terrorist police, DIGOS, at Milan's Questura (police headquarters).

Police forces all over the world—and especially in Europe—are being challenged by terrorist groups recruited in the Middle East by radical forces intent on destroying Western governments and cultures. The tragic bombings and heavily armed assaults on innocent civilians in France and Belgium are the latest and most deadly attacks.

Italy is at the center of the attempt to neutralize this threat with sophisticated police techniques and coordination among European governments. *No One Sleeps* is the fictionalization of the attempt by a cell of radical Muslims in Milan intent on attacking an important Italian cultural institution and killing hundreds of innocent Italians. When DIGOS, the Italian anti-terrorism police, learns about a possible clandestine terrorist cell, they send a team of top agents to discover who they are and stop them before they act.

Here is the opening chapter of *No One Sleeps* when a low level inspector at the port of La Spezia confesses to his brother-in-law, a police detective, that he has been taking bribes to allow shipments of suspicious cargo from Karachi, Pakistan, bound for Milan to pass through the port without being inspected.

This is how the story begins . . .

NO ONE SLEEPS

CHAPTER ONE

JUNE 22, 2013

The note read simply:

Marco, I'm in trouble. I'm worried about my family. Can we meet Sunday morning for coffee at Caffè Cavour? Gianni

Agent Marco Molinari stared at the note from his brother-in-law. It had been hand-delivered to the duty officer at the La Spezia Polizia di Stato headquarters, where Marco worked. The sealed white envelope had Marco's name scrawled on the front by a pen running out of ink. It looked like Gianni was in a hurry.

Marco was puzzled as to why Gianni had sent a note to the Questura instead of calling if his family was in danger. Strange. The reference to Gianni's family was disturbing; Gianni was married to Marco's sister, Elisabetta. Betta and Gianni had two young children, seven-year-old Anita and three-year-old Davide.

Gianni was a midlevel customs agent at the La Spezia port, between Genova and Pisa on Italy's northwestern coast along the Ligurian Sea. La Spezia was an important commercial port and arsenal for the Italian Navy. Gianni was assigned to the port's inspection unit, which off-loaded and inspected shipping containers arriving from ports in the Mediterranean, Asia, and the Middle East.

Marco reread the brief note, stuck it in his coat pocket, and headed to the parking lot behind the police station. When Marco reached his car, he took out his cell phone and punched Gianni's cell number. Marco had to find out if this was an emergency that needed immediate attention. As an experienced police officer, he was trained to be suspicious.

Gianni answered after one ring. "Pronto, ciao, Marco."

"Ciao, Gianni. Are you having dinner?"

The background noise of the family dinner table answered Marco's question. Three-year-old Davide was banging his fork on a plate and screaming, "No, no! Don't want, Mamma!"

Marco visualized the chaotic dinner scene that he had experienced on visits to their apartment: Betta struggling to feed Davide while he jerked his head left and right, pushing her hand away, food flying across the table and onto the floor.

Little Davide was a problem child, prone to outbursts. He was aggressive around other children, and he often fell down and screamed when he didn't get his way. He had an emotional condition that doctors hadn't identified yet. Davide's behavior was a strain on anyone who encountered him, especially his family and neighbors.

In the background, a TV was blaring an irksome commercial offering low, low rates for cell phone service. It bothered Marco that Betta's family ate with the TV on in the kitchen, a noisy distraction that added to the chaos.

"Yes," Gianni answered. "I didn't expect you to call so soon."

"I have your note. You should have called if you needed to talk right away. Are you in danger?"

"No, no, not right now. But I have to talk to you."

"Should I come over now?"

"No. It can wait until Sunday. Can we meet Sunday?"

"Of course. Are you sure it can wait? Your note worried me."

Gianni said something, but his words were drowned out by Davide's high-pitched wail in the background and the sound of him banging his fork on his plate. Marco could hear Betta trying to calm Davide down and taking him out of his high chair—he still had to be restrained in one, even at his age. "Davide, Davide . . . shush, shush . . . good boy. . . . Let's go in your bedroom . . . find your pajamas . . . so we can play before bedtime."

The kitchen TV blared another commercial of a weekend sale on summer clothes for children, the announcer bellowing about low prices and clothes that children needed to be popular with their playmates, and promoting Disney Princess and Ninja Turtles schoolbags, Spider-Man's cool diaries and Winx's pencil cases that children would need for school at the end of the summer.

Gianni said, "Davide's been sick all week. Betta called me this afternoon to come home and help her. He's been fussy, not letting her change his diaper, crying all day, refusing to nap."

"I hope he recovers soon," Marco said, distressed about his sister's family problems, which seemed to only get worse, never better. "It's hard when you have a sick child."

Gianni sighed. "It's been one thing after another. Davide had a cold and the flu in May and fell out of his bed one night and bruised his head. Last week someone pushed him off a swing in the park, and Betta had to rush him to the hospital. Poor Betta; she hasn't had a break in so long. It's so hard on us when Davide is not in kindergarten. Thank God Anita is going to the public summer school."

"Yes, I know Betta is worn out. About your note, Gianni, are you sure you want to wait until Sunday? What about tomorrow? I could come to your apartment."

"No, tomorrow isn't good. I'm taking care of the children while Betta has an appointment with her gyno. She hasn't gone since Davide was born. She's been neglecting her health to take care of the kids. Betta said I can have an hour Sunday morning. I will pick Michele up at noon and bring him to the apartment for the day."

Michele was Gianni's twelve-year-old son from an earlier marriage. Gianni had gotten his girlfriend pregnant in high school, and their marriage had lasted only five years. After a nasty divorce, Gianni had been left with monthly child support payments to Michele's mother. It was no secret how stressful it was for Gianni's family when Michele came every other weekend. Michele resented it that his father had another family whose children were too young to play with. To add to the stress, Michele was going through puberty, becoming emotional and moody. There were frequent arguments when he spent the day, with lots of shouting, arguing, and slamming of doors until Gianni took him to a video arcade or the park to kick a soccer ball around.

"I can make it Sunday morning at ten."

"Yes, thank you," Gianni said, his voice anxious.

"I'll see you then," Marco said. "Give my love to Betta and your kids. We'll get everyone together soon."

On his drive home to Costa di Murlo, Marco played back the hurried conversation with Gianni. Marco wasn't surprised about Gianni's note; he had suspected something was going on. His sister had confided to him that Gianni had been acting strangely the last couple weeks, moody and depressed. Some nights after work, he'd go for walks alone or stay in their bedroom with the door closed.

Marco had observed Gianni's withdrawn behavior when the family had come over for Betta's birthday in May. Marco's wife, Serena, had prepared a typical Ligurian menu: trofie pasta with pesto; leek and potato pie; zucchini stuffed with meat, cheese, ham, and grated bread; homemade focaccia; *cima alla Genovese;* lemon and pine nuts cake. She had put a bouquet of fresh flowers on the table and had presents for Betta, as well as gifts for Davide and Anita.

While Betta and Serena had talked in the kitchen, Marco had kept an eye on the kids playing by their pool on the patio. Gianni had spent the afternoon slouched on the sofa, drinking beer and watching a soccer match between AC Spezia Calcio and Carrarese on Tele Liguria Sud. When Marco had tried to engage him in conversation, Gianni had answered in one or two sentences, barely taking his eyes off the TV.

Marco knew Gianni had serious financial problems. Gianni supported two families on a modest customs officer's salary. He had even asked Marco for money when his landlord threatened to evict them if they didn't pay their back rent. It was a sad situation; Marco felt helpless, knowing his sister was struggling with a difficult marriage, a child with emotional problems, and constant money worries.

A once attractive, vivacious young woman, Betta now looked harried and worried, with rings under her eyes and stringy, uncombed hair. She dressed in clothes that should have gone to charity.

If only Betta had not met Gianni . . . had finished university . . . and had found a loving man with a good job and a promising future.

But what did Gianni mean when he said he was worried about his family?

* * * * *

Later that evening, Marco and Serena were on the deck of their hillside apartment overlooking La Spezia's harbor, sipping chilled Sciacchetrà from Cinque Terre after dinner while their children paddled in the little pool next to Serena's herb garden. Marco had given her Gianni's note and told her about the stressful conversation while Davide was throwing a temper tantrum.

Serena studied the note as Marco gazed at the fiery orange sun ball descending across the azure Ligurian Sea.

Sparrows and other songbirds were swirling overhead, settling in the eucalyptus trees and oleander bushes as the evening air cooled and crickets chirped in the garden. It was a peaceful end of a hot, humid summer day.

"That poor family," Serena said, laying down the note. "Every day they have a new crisis. It grieves me. I don't know what to say. They have so many problems . . . poor little Davide; I think he's autistic or has Asperger's syndrome. How are they going to handle that as he grows up? Poor Anita seems lost; all her parents' attention goes to Davide. She needs more affection; she seems needy. Betta is overwhelmed, trying to be a nurse, mother, and wife, with little support from Gianni. Michele's weekend visits all end in disaster, with the children crying, Betta and Gianni arguing, and Michele scowling and angry. He can be so mean. Do you know what he called Betta one night when he was leaving? He called her *'brutta puttana.'* The nerve of that dreadful boy! I don't see how Betta can put up with all the chaos."

"What can we do?" Marco said. "I've given them money. We see them once a month . . . what else is there? I feel hopeless. My heart aches for Betta . . . and the children."

Serena changed the subject. "What kind of trouble is Gianni worried about? Is it serious, something legal, or just family problems? Their marriage is in trouble; we know that. Is there something else?"

"It probably is serious," Marco said with a sigh. "But I don't think he wants to talk about their marriage. God, I hope he's not losing his job. What a disaster that would be."

Serena pressed her lips together and then sighed. "Could be. . . . Poor Betta."

* * * * *

Marco was at the Caffè Cavour at ten o'clock on that hot Sunday morning, sipping cappuccino and reading the weekend *Corriere della Sera.* He was seated at an outside table under an umbrella near Piazza Garibaldi, where he could see Gianni approach from any direction.

It was the usual Sunday morning parade on the sun-blazed piazza: young mothers pushing prams with toddlers wearing sun hats, walking in groups of two or three, alternating talking and texting on cell phones; male pensioners following shorthaired terriers and dachshunds on leashes; widowed *nonnas* strolling in short-sleeved black dresses, linking arms with each other, stooped over with age and from lifetimes of raising children and grandchildren. Some of them were huddled under umbrellas against the intense sunlight.

Marco glanced at his watch. Gianni was late. Typical. At ten thirty-five, Marco ordered another cappuccino. When he returned to his table, he spotted Gianni hurrying into the piazza from behind the *chiesa* where he'd likely parked his car, near the primary school.

Gianni's head shifted nervously left and right as he approached Caffè Cavour. He looked like he'd just gotten out of bed and grabbed clothes off the floor; his wrinkled shirt was untucked, the front drooping over his belt. Gianni's running shoes had tattered laces. His uncombed hair poked from under a cap. He hadn't shaved for a couple of days.

Marco rose and pushed a chair towards Gianni. *"Ciao, Gianni. Come va?"* Gianni refused the chair and motioned to the café. "Let's go inside. It's too hot outside," he said, his voice tense. His left hand was twitching like an electrical current had jabbed his elbow. "The air conditioner in my car isn't working."

Gianni hurried past Marco into the café, went to a corner table, and sat where he could see everyone in the café, on the patio, and on the piazza.

Marco ordered an espresso at the bar and brought the cup and saucer to the table. "Thank you," Gianni said, avoiding Marco's eyes as he sipped the inky-black espresso. Abruptly he said, "Let's go outside. I need a smoke." He tipped his head back, drained the bitter coffee, and set the cup on the tiny saucer.

"I thought you wanted to be inside—" Marco said, but Gianni had already risen and pushed back his chair.

Marco followed Gianni and found an empty table in the shade of one of the café's umbrellas. It was hot and muggy, 38°C already. People were staying in the shade of trees or awnings around the piazza.

Gianni reached into his back pocket and pulled out a Marlboro Rossa tobacco pouch and Rizla cigarette papers. He pinched brown flakes out of the package and dropped them into the paper, with some falling next to his saucer. He rolled the flakes in the paper, creased the ends together, and licked them before popping the rolled stump between his lips. He lit his lumpy cigarette with a plastic lighter, inhaled deeply, and then exhaled smoke over his shoulder.

Marco disliked smoking, believing it was a filthy, dangerous habit and an insult to people forced to breathe nearby. "You look tired, Gianni," Marco said, sipping his cappuccino, wishing Gianni would take off his sunglasses. "Did you sleep last night?"

Gianni took off his sunglasses, revealing bloodshot eyes that made him look older and world-weary. "Not much," he grunted. "Betta was up with Davide most of the night; he was coughing, crying. I got up a couple times to take care of him but then couldn't go back to sleep. I'll need a nap this afternoon."

"Davide's been sick a lot, hasn't he? How's Betta handling the stress? I've left messages for her, but she doesn't seem to have time to call back."

"It's not her fault. She's busy day and night. She needs rest, but I don't know how or when that can happen." He made a fluttering wave with his hand as if brushing away a fly.

Marco watched Gianni, his fingers twitching as he rolled the cigarette around. "What's going on, Gianni? Your note worried me."

Gianni picked a piece of tobacco off his lip and flicked it on the ground, avoiding Marco's eyes. He glanced furtively at people walking by in the shade, then again stood, motioning with his head that it was time to leave.

Gianni walked into the piazza and tossed his cigarette butt into the gravel path, glancing nervously in one direction, then another. Marco followed behind. Gianni meandered around the statue of Garibaldi, the hero of Italy's Risorgimento, mounted on his horse, leading his Redshirts into battle. He glanced up at the statue of the former sea captain who had left politics and moved to Sardinia to raise cattle. Gianni had told Marco once that Garibaldi was his personal hero; Gianni had even named his daughter after Garibaldi's wife, Anita.

Gianni looked away and strolled around the monument, which was on a stone plinth in a small circular garden with pink and white petunias enclosed by a wooden fence.

Marco followed a half-step behind his brother-in-law, observing his odd behavior, like that of a man seeking to run away and hide from strangers. Marco pointed to a corner of the piazza shaded by trees. "There's an empty bench over there," he said.

Their shoes crunched on the gravel path, kicking up dust and dried leaves. Neither spoke until they were seated in the shade.

Gianni took out his Marlboro Rossa packet again to roll another cigarette. "I'm in trouble, Marco," Gianni said. "Big trouble."

"Tell me."

Gianni lit the cigarette, took a long drag, and exhaled to his side. "I made a big mistake," he began, almost blurting out his confession. "A guy—Indian or a Paki, I couldn't tell—came up to me a couple months ago when I got home. He was nicely dressed . . . spoke perfect Italian with a Genovese accent. He knew my name. He asked me if I wanted to make some easy money. Fast. I was suspicious."

"You should have walked away."

Gianni spoke in a staccato fashion, like he wanted to rush through his pathetic tale. "He asked how Betta and the kids were. I was shocked. How would he know my family? He knew the school where Anita goes. He knew Betta took Davide to the park every morning. How did he know that? I was going to walk away . . . then he asked if I could use some extra money to buy new clothes for Betta and the kids."

"He probably had been spying on you for some time. What was his name?"

"He called himself Mimmo, but I didn't believe him. It's probably just an Italian nickname he uses."

"Foreigners often use phony Italian nicknames."

"But his Italian was good. He talked fast. He was only there about five minutes. He said he wanted to help my family."

"How much did he offer you?"

Gianni narrowed his eyes, avoiding looking at Marco. When he answered, it was with a hushed voice. "Five thousand euros. For an hour's work."

Marco balled his hands into fists. He was furious with Gianni but didn't want him to know. Bribing a customs official was a police matter, not just a family issue. "That's a lot of money, Gianni. He offered you a bribe."

Gianni took another drag, averting his eyes. "I know. Damn it, I should have walked away."

"What did he want you to do?"

Gianni closed his eyes for a moment, sweat glistening on his forehead. When he answered, he spoke in bursts, making Marco believe he hadn't confided in anyone about the incident that had likely caused him sleepless nights while he had suffered in silence.

"A container ship was coming into the harbor in a few days. He knew I was on a team that inspected containers. He wanted me to sign papers for one container without inspecting one of the boxes in it. He knew about the paperwork, who has to sign it. He knew my supervisor's name and even showed me a copy of his signature. I was shocked that he knew so much."

"Where was it going?"

"Milano."

"What did you do?"

Gianni grimaced like he'd bitten into a lime. "I . . . I did as he said. It was easy. My supervisor signed the papers I gave him, and the container was taken to the warehouse and left on the truck a couple days later."

"What was in the shipment?"

"I didn't ask."

Marco was stunned. Gianni had committed a serious crime that could send him to prison. But why had he taken so long to tell him? "You took a bribe, Gianni. You could lose your job and be in trouble with the police."

Gianni sucked his cigarette hard, ash falling on his soiled shoes. "I know . . . but the money . . . you know we don't have much. Betta doesn't work. Two young children take a lot of money. I pay support for Michele. I'm always broke. If it wasn't for the money my father gives me, we'd be living on the street." He blinked away tears, reaching up to wipe his eyes.

"Why did you wait to tell me? We could have arrested this criminal."

Gianni grimaced, looking like he had painful gas in his stomach. "There's more," he continued, speaking rapidly. "Mimmo came back a month later. Same deal. Another envelope with five thousand euros. Another shipment. Just look the other way and sign the documents. He asked if Betta was okay, as he hadn't seen her recently. He was watching our apartment. She was at your mother's in Parma for a couple days. Remember? Serena was there as well."

"I remember." Gianni's story was getting more complicated; he had apparently taken another bribe. Where did this end?

"The shipment came. I signed the paper and gave it to my supervisor, who signed without reading it. The container was put in a warehouse for delivery. It was also going to Milano. I felt guilty, but I'd already spent the money he'd given me before. I was tempted by the money."

"Everyone has a price, Gianni," Marco said, restraining his anger. He had to hear the rest of the story, which he suspected was more incriminating for Gianni. "Some people are corrupted by money. For others it's sex, a new car, a promotion, or a better job. People are tempted by what they don't have."

Gianni nodded, head lowered. He dropped his cigarette onto the gravel and squashed it with his shoe.

"What was in the shipment? You had the manifest."

"The paperwork said bicycle parts and clothes from China. Machine parts from Pakistan."

"There was something else in there."

"I know, but I didn't inspect."

"Does Betta know what you did?"

"No!" he said, raising his head, reacting as if he'd been slapped on the face. "If she did, she'd kill me! She's angry with me . . . we're . . . having problems. Marital problems. I'm sure she's told you."

Marco leaned back and took a moment before he answered. Betta had mentioned that Gianni had been acting strangely the last few weeks, distant and sullen. But he didn't want to let Gianni know Betta was confiding in him. "She did mention that you were worried about something. I called you a month ago, but you didn't return my call."

"I'm know. I'm sorry. I was afraid to tell you. But after . . . this week . . . I knew I had to see you."

Marco blinked. There was more. "What happened?"

Gianni looked away, pinching his forearm with his fingers like he wanted to rip off his skin. He reached for his Marlboro Rossa package but then stopped, stuffing it back into his pocket. "Mimmo was back Tuesday."

"Another bribe?"

Gianni shook his head. "Not a bribe. A threat."

"What did he say?"

"He asked if I thought Anita was safe at her school. He said that the walls around the playground have a breach; someone could reach in and grab a child. He was trying to scare me, Marco. And he did. I was terrified! Someone grabbing Anita? I couldn't sleep for nights after that."

Marco held his breath. He and Serena loved Anita almost like their own child. Serena was Anita's godmother. They had been at the hospital when she was born and had taken care of her so Gianni and Betta could have a weekend vacation before Davide was born. "You should have called me immediately. I could have had an officer there in minutes. We could have arrested him."

"It happened so fast. I was angry, and I was afraid for the kids. I wanted to hit him. He said another shipment was coming next week. If I didn't let it through, something might happen to Betta or one of the kids."

A warm breeze from the harbor rustled the towering palm trees in the park, making a soft scratching sound above their heads. A dried palm frond drifted to the ground, landing at Marco's feet. Marco was furious at what he was hearing: his brother-in-law admitting he had taken bribes, his family threatened. Possibly Marco's own sister's life was in danger. How could Gianni have been so foolish?

"You're in trouble, Gianni. So is your family."

"Can you help me, Marco, please?" he begged, finally looking at Marco, tears running down his cheeks into his scruffy, unshaven beard. "I don't know what to do." He wiped tears away with a knuckle, embarrassed by his confession. He lowered his head into his hands, leaned over, and started to sob.

Marco took out his cell phone. "I'm going to call the vice questore immediately. He might want to send an officer to your apartment to see if this Mimmo comes back. But you have to tell your story to a prosecutor."

Gianni made a sorrowful moan, like he'd been kicked in the belly. "Oh, no . . . do I really—"

"Yes. And you're coming to the Questura with me tomorrow for questioning. We'll need a statement about everything you told me."

Gianni uttered another moaning wail, turning away from Marco so he couldn't see his face.

* * * * *

Jack Erickson is the author or thrillers, mysteries, and romantic suspense novels. He is a former US Senate speechwriter, editor, and publisher of RedBrick Press books about the early days of the craft brewing industry. His first book, "Star Spangled Beer: A History to America's New Microbreweries and Brewpubs," became a classic and was named the best self-published book in 1987.

Erickson travels extensively in Italy and spends summers in Milan researching his thrillers. He lives in northern California with his wife.

Erickson's books are available on your ereader, smartphone, or tablet.

Sign up for his newsletter here:

www.jackerickson.com

www.ingramcontent.com/pod-product-compliance
Lightning Source LLC
Chambersburg PA
CBHW050446110726
47899CB00003B/828